THE HANGMAN

Death stalks through the residential district of Hill Green, carrying off two prominent members of the community in two days. The first is a man found hanging from a lamp-post; the second, a young woman found hanging from a beam in the roof of a barn. When found, both corpses have a small card pinned to their clothing, bearing the same pencilled message: WITH THE COMPLIMENTS OF THE HANGMAN. Detective-Inspector Shadgold of Scotland Yard soon realises this is going to be one of his toughest cases . . .

GERALD VERNER

THE HANGMAN

Complete and Unabridged

LINFORD
Leicester

First published in Great Britain in 1934

First Linford Edition
published 2015

*A catalogue record for this book is available
from the British Library.*

ISBN 978–1–4448–2377–6

Published by
F. A. Thorpe (Publishing)
Anstey, Leicestershire

Set by Words & Graphics Ltd.
Anstey, Leicestershire
Printed and bound in Great Britain by
T. J. International Ltd., Padstow, Cornwall

This book is printed on acid-free paper

TO
VI WITH LOVE

Contents

1

The Surrey Murderer

Most people have heard of that big rambling red-brick building nestling among the Berkshire hills, which is called Widemoore Asylum, and which houses those unfortunate people who have been classified by law as the criminally insane. Looked at casually from the road, it has the appearance of a country residence owned by some wealthy family, rather than a Government Institution. Its lawns are trim and well kept; its flower beds blaze with colour, and its hedges are symmetrical and closely clipped. Only the steel bars that can be seen guarding some of the windows betray its real purpose; the segregation from the rest of the world of those unfortunate creatures who due to some kink of the brain have violently taken human life. For the majority of the people incarcerated within those pleasant

1

walls have been convicted of murder, and found by a merciful jury 'guilty but insane.'

On a warm morning in late February, when the trees were beginning to show signs of awakening from their winter sleep and donning their summer finery, Colonel Hastings, the governor of this establishment, sat behind his big desk in the large airy room which served him for an office, and from which he controlled the lives of those committed to his care, and stared out of the window across the broad expanse of lawn that lay within his view. His face, florid and inclined to fatness, wore a worried expression, and his large capable hands played nervously with a pen, rolling it gently up and down the blotting-pad, while his lips beneath his grey closely-cropped moustache, pursed themselves into a silent whistle. His whole appearance betrayed doubt and a certain vague uneasiness. For some minutes he sat staring fixedly out upon the green of the grass plot, and then with a sudden shrug of his broad shoulders, he leaned back in his padded chair, reached towards a box of cigarettes, took one and lit it. He inhaled the smoke deeply, expelling it in a slow stream from between his still pursed lips, and shook his head. There came a tap at the door, and without looking round, Hastings grunted an invitation to enter. A dark, pleasant-looking man came in, and approached the desk, carrying a handful of papers. His round eyes twinkled through the thick lens of the horn-rimmed glasses he wore perched on the bridge of his rather large nose.

'If you will sign these, sir,' he said, laying the papers on the blotting-pad, 'everything will be in order.'

The governor picked up his pen without a word and brought the nib towards the line which awaited his signature. With it almost touching the paper he paused.

'I don't like it, Thompson,' he muttered uneasily. 'I don't like it at all.'

His secretary raised his eyebrows slightly.

'You cannot alter the law, sir,' he replied, 'however much you may disagree with it. The whole thing has been approved by the Home Secretary and there it is.'

'Nevertheless it's a tremendous responsibility,' said Colonel Hastings. 'Think,

Thompson, we are letting this man loose on the world, a man who has already taken two lives, a man who has been proved to possess a homicidal kink.'

'It's not your responsibility, sir,' argued Thompson, 'all the necessary formalities have been complied with. Smedley has been examined by four specialists, and they have all reported him completely sane. The mania from which he suffered has been cured.'

'How can they be sure of that?' demanded Hastings vehemently. 'How can they tell he won't break out again? They can't! The first that anyone will know of it is when the unfortunate victim is found.'

Thompson shrugged his shoulders.

'I quite agree with you, sir,' he said. 'But as I remarked before, the law is the law and you can't go against it. This man, who is undoubtedly a murderer, was not responsible for his actions. He was insane but he has now become sane, and therefore according to the law he can no longer be detained.'

The governor sighed.

'Oh well, I suppose it's no business of mine,' he muttered, and scrawled his signature at the foot of the three documents that lay before him. 'When is he going?'

'To-morrow morning,' answered Thompson, gathering up the papers. 'His relations are sending for him.'

'"The Surrey Murderer," the newspapers called him,' said Hastings musingly. 'He hanged his wife and little daughter. Twenty-years ago, that was, and now we're letting him out to hang some more people.'

'Aren't you being rather pessimistic, sir?' said the secretary, smiling.

'Maybe I am, Thompson, maybe I am,' replied the governor, rising to his feet. 'But I don't believe in letting these people go. Once a lunatic always a lunatic is my motto. However, as you say, it's not my responsibility, thank God.'

It worried him all the same for the rest of the day, and a greater part of the night, for he slept badly. At twelve o'clock on the following morning, a big saloon car arrived, and into it, after certain formalities had been complied with, stepped Harold Smedley, accompanied by the brother who had come to take him away.

Colonel Hastings watched the car as it disappeared round a bend in the broad drive, and returned to his duties a silent and thoughtful man.

'Are you still worrying about Smedley, sir?' asked Thompson during the afternoon, noticing his employer's obvious preoccupation.

'To be perfectly candid, I am,' confessed the colonel. 'I've got a premonition that we haven't heard the last of him. I think we've done a very foolish thing, and — well I don't mind admitting that I'm afraid.'

It was not until a year later that his fears were realized.

2

The Thing on the Lamp-post

It is a remarkable fact that the enmity which exists between the various residential districts surrounding London proper should amount almost to racial hatred. But it is so. The inhabitants of Golders Green regard the residents of Tooting with a scornful eye, the elect of Chelsea speak about the denizens of Balham with curled lips as though they were an unnecessary evil. Mayfair shrugs its thin shoulders when Brixton is mentioned and murmurs: 'My dear, too frightfully surburban.' And Bloomsbury looks on everyone that lives outside its own small circle with rank suspicion. But by far the worst cases of this district snobbery are to be found in the people who live in the innumerable 'Garden Cities' which have recently sprung up with all the rapid growth of unchecked weeds in a neglected garden. These people carry the matter into the realms of a fine art. Their particular corner of the world is the only place where any decent-minded person could possibly live. People who inhabit other neighbourhoods exist but do not live. They merely make the best of a bad job and are to be pitied. Nowhere was this extraordinary attitude of mind more notice-able than among the residents of Hill Green. This, according to the advertisements, 'most desirable residential district,' is within twenty minutes of London. To those who possess cars, this is probably true, but otherwise the statement is — to say the least of it — exaggerated. It is a fact that trains run frequently from the station at Hill Green to Waterloo, and vice versa, and that if they made a non-stop run, they would probably do the journey in twenty min-utes. Unfortunately they do not make a non-stop run. There is a signal-box out-side Hill Green Station, containing a malicious signalman whose one apparent joy in life is to stop the train after it has left Hill Green, and keep it impatiently waiting, for at least ten minutes before he reluc-tantly allows it to continue its journey.

Such, however, is the loyalty of the residents that they invariably refer to the excellence of the train service at Hill Green, and contrast it, to their detriment, with the train services from other districts.

Mr. Percy Stott was enlarging upon this to his friend, Mr. Julian Rusk, as the seven-twenty train entered the straight run that ended at the flower-decked platform of Hill Green. He began it by extracting his watch, a large and important affair, from his waistcoat pocket, and peered at it through his rimless pince-nez, with great concentration.

'You see, Julian,' he remarked impressively.

'Twenty-seven and a half minutes since we left Waterloo, and we're just on there. Pretty good, eh?'

'I thought you said it only took twenty minutes,' answered Mr. Rusk, a short, stout and jovial little man who was head cashier in the firm which Mr. Stott graced in the capacity of under-manager.

'So it does, usually,' said Mr. Stott. 'I have done the journey in fifteen. We should have done it in twenty to-night, if we hadn't had that signal against us.'

He did not add that the signal was against them five nights out of six, or that the occasion, a memorable one, when the journey had been accomplished in fifteen minutes, was the opening of the new line when everything had been done to facilitate speed.

The train slid along the platform, and screeched to a standstill. The doors began to swing open, and discharge the fortunate passengers who lived in this ante-room to Heaven, including Mr. Stott and Mr. Rusk.

'Notice the difference in the air, Julian?' asked Mr. Stott with pride as though the air at Hill Green was his special monopoly. 'Keen and fresh. None of your London smoke here.'

Mr. Rusk grunted and wiped away a large smut which had attached itself to the bridge of his nose. They joined the throng of people streaming along the platform towards the exit gate. Mr. Stott showed his season, and Mr. Rusk gave up his ticket to the sleepy-eyed official who was there for that purpose, and they turned and crossed the iron bridge over the line.

They emerged from the entrance to the station into the cold frosty air of the night.

'I live about ten minutes' walk from here,' said Mr. Stott, as he turned to the left, and set off briskly along the road. 'Up on Milton's Rise. Wonderful view from the back windows, old man. You won't be able to see it to-night, but you'll see it in the morning. Right across the golf course.'

Mr. Rusk grunted again, his breath issuing from his mouth in little gushes of steamy vapour, as his fat legs strove to keep pace with the longer strides of his friend.

'If you ever think of moving, you ought to come and live at Hill Green,' continued Mr. Stott. 'Just suit Mrs. Rusk. I've never felt so well in my life before. Since I came here I've put on nearly a stone.'

This was not a very good recommendation so far as Mr. Rusk was concerned, since he spent a large proportion of his leisure in trying to remove several stones. But so full of enthusiasm was Mr. Stott over the advantages of Hill Green that this never occurred to him.

'Nice lot of people live here, too,' he went on as they began to ascend a rather steep hill. 'Mostly professional men and their families. Select, you know what I mean? Not the sort of place where you find every Tom, Dick or Harry.'

'How long have you been here now?' asked Mr. Rusk, a trifle breathlessly.

'Getting on for eleven months,' answered his friend. 'I'm buying the house, you know, through the Hill Green Estate Trust. Very reasonable terms, too, they gave me. In another forty years it'll be my own property. If you ever think of coming here, you couldn't do anything better than go to them. There's a house on the Rise that would just suit you.'

Mr. Rusk muttered something about having several years of his lease still to run, and ventured to inquire, feeling rather cold, how much farther they had to go.

'Only a step now,' said Mr. Stott cheerily. 'I rather enjoy the walk to and from the station. It does you good, you know. Blows the cobwebs away in the morning, and gets some of the city smoke out of your lungs at night!'

They reached the top of the hill, and turned right into a short straight road, on one side of which were finished houses, and on the other heaps of slates, and bricks and half-reared walls.

'We turn to the left at the end of this road,' said Mr. Stott, 'cross Oak Apple Lane and then we're home.'

'Um!' said Mr. Rusk, wondering what his friend's definition of a step was.

'The Rise starts on the other side of the lane,' explained Mr. Stott. 'So we shan't be long, and Mrs. Stott will have something hot all ready for us.'

'Um!' said Mr. Rusk, again with greater emphasis.

'It's a bit dark here, as you can see,' his friend went on; 'they haven't got the street lamps up yet, but the Rise is different. That's all finished. That's why I chose my house there. These new houses' — he waved his hand towards the partially-constructed side of the road — 'are nearly all damp, you know. Dangerous to take one of them until they've had time to air, as you might say.'

Mr. Rusk, whose soul was longing for a fire and a hot meal, vaguely agreed with him.

They reached the end of the street, and came to the suddenly rural Oak Apple Lane, bordered by clumps of trees and mist-swathed fields. Crossing it they entered a narrow footpath between high hedges, and came out at the foot of a long, straight stretch of road that sloped sharply upwards.

'This,' said Mr. Stott, proudly, 'is Milton's Rise.'

'Very nice too,' said Mr. Rusk, though whether he was referring to the beauties of Milton's Rise, or merely to the fact that they had got there at last, was known only to himself.

They began to breast the steep slope.

'You see,' said Mr. Stott, pointing ahead, 'this part is well lighted.'

Mr. Rusk looked at the two lamp-posts set at two hundred yards from each other, and offered no comment.

They continued to ascend the incline.

'My little place,' began Mr. Stott, 'is right at the top. You can — '

'What is *that*?' Mr. Rusk's voice was suddenly shrill and unnatural and his extended arm shook a little.

'What is what?' said his friend, who was rather short sighted.

'That?' quavered Mr. Rusk. 'God Almighty! It's a man!'

It was a man, or rather it had once been a man. Now it was nothing but a limp and unpleasant object that dangled hideously from the arm of the first lamp-post.

Mr. Stott clutched his companion's wrist and stared.

'It *is* a man!' he breathed hoarsely. 'A dead man!'

'Ought — oughtn't we to do something?' muttered Mr. Rusk. 'He may — he may not be quite dead.'

Mr. Stott made unintelligible sounds in his throat, and together they advanced, covering the few yards that separated them from the lamp-post and its ghastly burden. The man's feet were barely six inches from the pavement, and the head fallen on to the shoulder showed the congested face. Mr. Stott, suppressing a shiver, looked up.

'I'm afraid he *is* dead,' he whispered. 'We'd — we'd better inform the police.

'There's something here,' interrupted Mr. Rusk sharply, 'look!'

He pointed to a patch of white that showed up with gleaming distinctness against the Thing's dark clothes. Mr. Stott bent forward and peered at it.

It was a small square card, and it had been pinned to the coat. On it, printed in capital letters, were the words:

'WITH THE COMPLIMENTS OF THE HANGMAN.'

3

The Second Victim

Major Payton looked across his desk at Inspector Lightfoot, read nothing in that individual's stolid face, and looked down at his blotting-pad. Presently he cleared his throat and shifted uneasily in his chair.

'Well?' he grunted at last.

'Well, sir?' said the inspector questioningly.

'What are we going to do?' asked the chief constable irritably.

'We are doing everything that's possible, sir,' was the reply. 'We are inquiring into the past life of the dead man in the hope of finding a motive for the crime.'

The other stopped with a gesture.

'I know. I know all that,' he said impatiently, 'but I doubt if it'll do any good. I knew Wallington very well, poor fellow. In fact, as I have told you he was a relation of mine, a cousin. I don't think you'll find anything out about him that'll help you.'

'There must be some sort of a motive, sir,' said the inspector, knitting his ginger eyebrows, and rubbing the lowest of his chins.

'Must there?' growled the chief constable. 'I'm not so sure in this case.'

The ginger eyebrows rose quickly into half-moons across the red forehead.

'What exactly do you mean, sir?' asked the inspector.

The chief constable leaned forward resting his elbows on the blotting-pad. His dark eyes under his smooth brows stared fully into the surprised blue ones opposite him.

'That card that was pinned to his coat,' he said slowly. 'That looks to me like the work of a lunatic. The Hangman!' He shook his head. 'It's all too sensational. Too unreal.'

Inspector Lightfoot crossed his legs.

'Maybe you're right, sir,' he said. 'Maybe you're not. I hope you're not, because if Doctor Wallington was murdered by a lunatic, it's going to make it

18

very, very difficult.'

'That's why I want to put a suggestion to you,' said Payton quickly. 'Don't you think we ought to call in the aid of the Yard?'

Lightfoot's eyebrows returned to their original frown, and the chief constable added hastily:

'I don't want you to think I doubt your ability to handle the affair, but — well it's a peculiar case. The newspapers will get hold of it and make a feature of it, and if we don't find out who killed Wallington they'll go for us for not asking the Yard for help.'

The inspector sighed. He knew that it would be a big case, and that the newspapers would be full of it, and he hoped that later on they would be full of him and how brilliantly he had handled the matter.

'You must do as you think best, sir,' he said, after a perceptible pause. 'It's entirely for you to decide. Personally I don't think the Yard can do any more than we're doing.'

The chief constable reached for a

cigarette and lit it. He pushed the box across the desk to Lightfoot, but the inspector shook his head and waited. He had not to wait long.

'I don't want to act precipitantly,' said Payton. 'If you think you can manage to bring this business to a successful conclusion, go ahead. But I'm warning you, if you fail they'll throw mud.'

'Let me try, sir,' said the inspector quickly.

The chief constable blew out a long and lingering cloud of smoke.

'All right,' he said, 'but don't forget that at the moment we've no more idea who killed Wallington than Adam.'

'I know, sir,' answered Lightfoot. 'I'm not likely to forget it.'

'We've got to do something, and quickly,' the chief constable went on. 'Now what are we *doing*?'

Inspector Lightfoot looked slightly embarrassed. He uncrossed his legs and then hurriedly recrossed them, coughing nervously.

'We're making the usual inquiries, sir,' he began.

'Keep that stuff for the papers, Lightfoot,' broke in Major Payton wearily. 'There's no need to try and work it on me! What have you definitely found out?'

'Nothing, sir,' answered Lightfoot candidly. 'Doctor Wallington, according to his housekeeper, was in his usual health, and was if anything more than usually cheerful all day, so the question of suicide — '

'Was there ever a question of suicide?' asked Payton. 'The poor fellow couldn't possibly have hanged himself to that lamp-post — apart from the card.'

'I was considering every possibility,' replied the inspector apologetically. 'It would have been difficult for Doctor Wallington to have hanged himself, but it would not have been impossible. He *could* have done it, and he *could* have written the card himself.'

'But why should he?' demanded the chief constable.

'Exactly, sir,' nodded the inspector. 'That's why I dismissed the idea of suicide as unlikely. As I was saying, sir, he was in the best of spirits all day, and shortly after dinner he went out saying he would be back at nine-thirty, when he was expecting a patient to call. He never came back. At seven-forty he was found hanging from the lamp-post on Milton's Rise by Mr. Stott and his friend.'

'What time did he leave his house?' asked the chief constable.

'At seven o'clock exactly,' replied Lightfoot.

'He must have had an early dinner,' muttered Payton.

'He did, sir,' said the inspector, 'he ordered it for six o'clock.'

'He left the house at seven,' muttered the chief constable, 'and at seven-forty he was found hanging from the lamp-post on Milton's Rise. Um! Forty minutes later.'

'Yes, sir,' nodded Lightfoot.

'You haven't been able to find out where he went at seven?' asked Payton. 'The fact that he ordered his dinner an hour earlier than usual looks as though he was going to keep an appointment.'

The inspector nodded again.

'Yes, sir, it does,' he agreed, 'but we haven't been able to find out who with, or where. I have a list of all his patients, and Sergeant Bolton is making inquiries among them to find out if there was an urgent case whom he was likely to be visiting.'

'I see.' The chief constable crushed out the stub of his cigarette in the ash-tray. 'Well, you seem to be doing all that can be done, Lightfoot, so for the time being you'd better carry on as best you can. For the Lord's sake, though, get hold of something definite as quickly as possible.'

'Yes, sir,' said Lightfoot. 'I'm going to — '

The telephone bell, raucous and insistent, drowned the end of his sentence. Major Payton reached for the instrument and held the receiver to his ear.

'Hello!' he said. 'Yes, Payton speaking. What's that? . . . Yes . . . Go on, man . . . Where? . . . What time? . . . Good God! All right, I'll send. Eh? What's that? Read that over again, will you . . . ?' With his free hand he picked up a pencil and scribbled on his blotting-pad. 'Right, I've got that . . . Yes, yes, we'll do what we can as quickly as we can . . . Ring off now, will you, and I'll let you have a word within a quarter of an hour.'

He hung up the receiver and looked at Lightfoot. His face was paler, and had suddenly become drawn and haggard. He was silent for so long that the inspector was forced to speak.

'What was that, sir?' he asked.

'That was Dilling,' said the chief constable. 'You know him, Lightfoot, the constable at Hill Green?'

'Yes, sir?' said Lightfoot, leaning forward in his chair in excitement. 'Yes, sir?'

'He was telephoning to tell me,' said Major Payton, speaking very slowly, 'that at nine-fifteen this morning a labourer in the employ of Farmer Leeman, of Hill Green, went to get some tools from a barn in one of Leeman's fields. He was surprised to find the lock smashed and the door ajar. He went in thinking that some tramp had broken into the barn, and stolen the tools that he had left there. As he entered he knocked against something — something that was hanging from the cross beam of the roof . . . ' The chief constable lowered his voice and passed his tongue over his dry lips . . . 'It was the body of a woman, Lightfoot, and she had been dead for some time.'

'Good God, sir!' The words came from the inspector like a small explosion. 'Another one!'

The chief constable nodded and his hands gripped the edge of his desk.

'Exactly, Lightfoot,' he said gruffly. 'Another one. To be exact, Miss Irene Mortimer, and' — he stared the inspector straight in the face — 'there was a card, Lightfoot, a small square card pinned to her coat,' his eyes dropped to his blotting-pad, 'on which had been printed in pencil: 'With the compliments of — ''

'The Hangman!' breathed the inspector, and the chief constable nodded.

4

Terror!

'ANOTHER HANGING MURDER
AT HILL GREEN.
'SECOND CRIME IN TWO DAYS.
'WHO IS THE HANGMAN?
'Hill Green, Saturday.

'Death has stalked through the pleasant residential district of Hill Green, and within two days carried off two prominent members of the community. Death in its most dreadful form — that of murder.

'Close upon the heels of the discovery of the dead body of Doctor Wallington, which was found hanging from a lamp-post on Milton's Rise at seven-forty on Thursday evening, comes a second and even more terrible tragedy. This morning at nine-fifteen the dead body of Miss Irene Mortimer was found hanging in a barn near Hayloft Farm. The discovery was made by Thomas Jay, a labourer in the employ of Mr. John Leeman, to whom the barn belongs. According to his own statement, Jay went to the barn with the object of getting some tools which he kept there, and which he wanted for his morning's work. To his surprise, he found that the lock had been broken and that the door was partly open. On entering he discovered, to his horror, the body of a woman hanging from a cross beam which supports the roof of the barn. Jay at once communicated with the police, and the dead woman was cut down. She was later identified as being Miss Irene Mortimer, of 10, Oaklands Road, Hill Green. Doctor Murford, the police surgeon, who examined the body, stated that death had taken place at least six hours before, and was due to asphyxiation. The crime was in every way identical with the killing of Doctor Wallington on Thursday evening last, even to the finding, pinned to the woman's clothing, of a card bearing the words: 'With the compliments of The Hangman,' printed in pencil. There can be little doubt that both murders are the work of the same hand. A wave of panic has swept over Hill Green and the surrounding district, and much speculation is rife as to whether this is the beginning to a series of outrages similar to the infamous Dusseldorf murders. There seems ample ground for this belief, since no motive has yet come to light to account for the tragic deaths of the two victims. Both were well known in Hill Green, and highly respected. Miss Mortimer was a spinster, and Doctor Wallington a bachelor. They both lived alone except for their servants, and were curiously enough distantly related, being cousins twice removed. The manner of the crimes and the cards found in both cases lead to the supposition that the murders are the work of a homicidal maniac. If this is the explanation, the police cannot be too expeditious in apprehending the criminal, for while he or she is at large nobody in the vicinity is safe.

'Later.

'Official inquiries under the direction of Inspector Lightfoot, who is in charge of both cases, have elicited the following facts:

'That the last known person to see Miss Mortimer alive is Mr. Cyril Haytor, of 14, Browning Road.

'That on the night previous to her death (Friday) Miss Mortimer was visiting friends at Mrs. Topliss', 6, The Crescent.

'That she left Mrs. Topliss' shortly after eleven-thirty, and was accompanied part of the way home by Mr. Haytor.

'That all her friends and acquaintances affirm that she was in excellent health, and seemed to have no premonition of the fatality that was to overtake her.

'In an interview with our representative, Mr. Cyril Haytor said:

' 'I was at Mrs. Topliss' with Miss Mortimer, and except for a slight depression due to the death of Doctor Wallington, she was in her usual spirits. When she left at eleven thirty-five, I offered to see her home. At the corner of Browning Road, which is where I live, she refused to allow me to go any farther, and after saying good night, we parted. She went off along Beech Avenue, and I went home. That is the last I saw of her.'

'It has been ascertained that Miss Mortimer never reached her house in Oaklands Road, which is a turning out of Beech Avenue. Between the time she left Mr. Haytor — approximately five to twelve — and the ten minutes it would have taken her to reach her own house, she must have met her murderer. How this person persuaded her to accompany him to the barn where her body was subsequently found, and which is nearly three quarters of a mile away, it is impossible to conjecture.

'But the obvious inference is that Miss Mortimer was not unacquainted with the man or woman whom she met between those two points, the corner of Browning Road and Number 10, Oaklands Road. At that hour of night she would not have stopped to speak to a stranger, and there are no signs on the body to indicate that she was attacked or drugged in any way. The whole thing is an impenetrable mystery, with only one possible solution. That somewhere at large in the neighbourhood is a dangerous lunatic, whose mania takes the form of a desire to kill. This person, male or female, may be outwardly normal in every way, and therefore the more difficult to apprehend. But for the safety of the community at large, and to avenge the deaths of the two unfortunate victims of this 'lust killer,' he must be apprehended and put safely under lock and key. It is essential that the police should use every endeavour to bring about this result as quickly as possible, and we earnestly recommend the calling in and co-operation of Scotland Yard without further delay.

'*Stop Press.*
'We understand that Major Payton, the chief constable for the district, has been in telephonic communication with London, and that a detective

from Scotland Yard can be expected to arrive very shortly to take charge of the campaign to run this unknown killer who calls himself 'The Hang-man' to earth.'

5

Shadgold Pays a Call

At five-thirty on that Saturday afternoon, Detective-Inspector Shadgold sat behind the big desk in his cheerless office at Scotland Yard, and debated with himself the advisability of going home. He had had a busy and rather unprofitable day, for a clue which he had been following up in connection with a minor case on which he was engaged had proved useless. He yawned and stretched himself, rose to his feet and looked out of the window. It was not a pleasant afternoon by any means, and he turned away from the dreary prospect with a grunt. A drizzle of rain was falling, and the roadway and pavements were wet and glistening. It would take him, by tube, half an hour to reach his home, but once there there would be food, a warm fire, slippers, and a glass of something to remove the chill of his journey. His square, red face brightened a little at the prospect, and he went over to where his hat and coat hung behind the door. One podgy hand was reaching up to take the coat from its hook when the telephone rang. It was the house telephone, not the ordinary one. Shadgold knew the difference in the tone of the bell. He went back to the desk and picked up the receiver. Holding it to his ear he listened to the voice that came over the wire, and frowned.

'All right, sir, I'll come at once,' he said, and replaced the receiver on its rack.

The frown deepened, clouding his previous cheerful expression. He crossed over to the door, opened it and went out into the stone corridor. Going to the end of this he descended a flight of stairs, walked half way along another passage, and stopped before a door, on which he tapped. A voice bade him come in, and he entered a large and comfortably-furnished office. At a rosewood writing-table a grey-haired man with remarkably keen dark eyes was seated.

'Sit down, Shadgold,' said the Assistant Commissioner, and waved his hand across a litter of papers towards an empty chair.

Shadgold seated himself rather uncomfortably on the extreme edge.

'I suppose you've read in the newspapers about this business at Hill Green,' went on the grey-haired man.

Shadgold nodded.

'Well,' continued the other, 'the chief constable has phoned for assistance, and I'm sending you down.'

'Yes, sir,' said Shadgold, the vision of his comfortable evening fading rapidly away. 'You want me to drop the Darnley business?'

'Yes, Arthurs can take that on,' said the Assistant Commissioner. 'Anybody can do that. But this Hill Green job isn't anybody's meat. It needs a good man.'

Shadgold's face became suffused with a pleasant flush at the implied compliment.

'Thank you, sir,' he said, 'but it's going to be a difficult job.'

'I agree with you,' replied the Assistant Commissioner, 'but do your best. Take two men and get off by car as quickly as you like. I've told them you're coming and they'll be expecting you. Who will you take with you?'

The inspector took a small engagement book from his waistcoat pocket and flicked the pages.

'Nares and Larson,' he said. 'They're not on anything special at the moment, sir.'

'Right, take them then,' said the grey-haired man. 'And for heaven's sake catch this lunatic or whoever it is before we start getting any questions asked in the House. In this case the county police have acted sensibly. They've asked us for help at once instead of waiting until they've made a mess of everything. I wish they'd always do it.'

'So do I, sir,' said Shadgold. 'Is there anything else, sir?'

The Assistant Commissioner shook his head.

'No,' he answered. 'They'll tell you all that is known about these crimes when you get down there.'

'Then I'll be getting along, sir,' said the inspector rising.

'Good luck!' said the Assistant Commissioner.

'Thank you, sir,' said Shadgold, and

went to the door.

With the handle in his hand, he was recalled.

'You'd better stay at Hill Green, I think,' said the grey-haired man. 'You and the men.'

Shadgold nodded.

'Yes, I think that's the best way, sir,' he agreed, and as the Assistant Commissioner turned once more to his papers, he made his exit.

Going back to his own office, he lighted a thin, black cigar and sat down at his desk. He had read everything that the newspapers had had to say about the Hill Green crimes, and he realized that he was up against a stiff proposition. Motiveless crime of any description is always difficult, for there is nothing to get hold of. The police rely to a very large degree on the motive to help them in their solution. So much so that it has become a standard saying at Scotland Yard 'that if you look after the motive the rest will take care of itself!' Here, at any rate up to the present, there was apparently no motive. There was also the distinct possibility that no motive would ever come to light — that the person responsible for the murders was insane. In that case there was the whole population of Hill Green and the surrounding district to choose from. The more he thought of it, the more he became convinced that it was not going to be an easy business, and although he was pleased at the compliment that had been paid him, he was beginning to wish that the powers that be had chosen somebody else. Drawing the telephone towards him, he got himself put through to the transport department, and arranged for a car to take him down to Hill Green. Having done this, he proceeded to arrange with Nares and Larson to accompany him. When he had finished these preliminaries he glanced at his watch. It was just on half-past six. In order to allow himself time for a meal he had ordered the police car for seven-thirty, but as he put on his hat and coat, with the intention of putting this idea into practice, a fresh one occurred to him, and with a slight lifting of the heavy frown that had settled on his brow ever since his interview with the Assistant Commissioner, he hurried from the Yard and hailed a taxi. Fifteen minutes later he was ringing the bell of a large house in Portland Place. To the elderly woman who answered his summons he put a question, and a little later was conducted up the stairs and ushered into a large room on the first floor. A man of middle height, with dark hair that was slightly grey at the temples, rose from a littered writing-table to greet him as he entered.

'How are you, Shadgold?' he said, holding out his hand. 'It's some time since I've seen anything of you. White was only wondering this morning what had become of you.'

'I've been pretty busy lately, Mr. Lowe,' said Shadgold, laying his hat down on the settee. 'Nothing big, but a thundering lot of little niggling affairs. And now just as I thought there was a chance of getting a little easier time, they've landed me with a real snorter.'

Trevor Lowe smiled. He had guessed that this sudden visit portended something unusual that Shadgold had come up against.

'Sit down and tell me all about it,' he said, pushing forward a chair. 'Will you have a drink?'

'Thanks, just a spot,' replied the inspector gratefully, sinking into the comfortable embrace of the chair.

The dramatist went over to the sideboard and poured out a stiff whisky. Carrying this back, he gave it to Shadgold.

'Now when you've got rid of that let's hear all about it,' he said.

Shadgold swallowed half the contents of the glass at a gulp, and set it down.

'It's this Hill Green business,' he explained. 'The locals have asked for help and the Yard's sending me down. I'm leaving at seven-thirty.'

The smile vanished from Lowe's face.

'You're going to find yourself up against a tough job,' he remarked.

'I know,' answered the inspector. 'It's going to be about the toughest I've ever tackled, and that's why — er — I thought — you see — I don't want to — ' He reddened and stopped.

'You want to know if I'll help you,' said Lowe. 'Is that it?'

'That's it, Mr. Lowe,' said Shadgold with a sigh of relief. 'I know it's a lot to ask and of course, if you're busy — '

'As a matter of fact, I'm not at the moment,' interrupted Lowe. 'I finished my new play last night, and I was intending to take a holiday. I've read all that the newspapers have to say about these murders, and I must admit that I am very much interested.'

Trevor Lowe's hobby, when he found time to indulge in it, was crime. He was intensely interested in police work, and it was during the time that he was engaged in writing a murder play that he had met Inspector Shadgold. He had gone to Scotland Yard in order to get some facts, regarding police procedure, and had been interviewed by the inspector. Shadgold was at the time investigating the murder of Thomas Carraway, the ex-member of Parliament who had been found stabbed to death in the grounds of his house in the country. He had discussed the case with Lowe, with the result that when he had found himself completely at sea, the dramatist had been able to suggest a theory which eventually solved the mystery. Since then he had taken a tremendous interest in any case with which Shadgold was concerned. They had worked together over the affair at Phantom Hollow,[1] and the other business connected with the murder of Elmer N. Jensen.[2]

'Well, if you'll give me a hand, I shall be very grateful, Mr. Lowe,' said the inspector.

'I know nothing more about the matter than I've read in the newspapers,' said Lowe, lighting a cigarette.

'Neither do I,' replied Shadgold. 'I shall probably hear some more when I arrive at Hill Green to-night — if there's anything they've kept back.' He reached out a hand and finished the remainder of his drink. 'As I said before,' he went on, 'I'm leaving at seven-thirty from the Yard. I suppose' — he hesitated — 'you couldn't come along too, if I called for you?'

'Not to-night,' Lowe shook his head.

---

[1] *Phantom Hollow*. (Wright & Brown.)
[2] *The Next to Die*. (Wright & Brown.)

'Besides, I don't think it would be good policy for us to go down together. These county people may put up with Scotland Yard, but I'm sure they'd resent a private individual butting in.'

'Let 'em go on resenting!' growled Shadgold. 'If you're there at my invitation —'

'It's not going to make things any easier for you,' ended Lowe. 'No, I'll tell you what I will do. I'll come down to-morrow during the morning, and if you'll let me know by phone where you'll be, we can meet and chat matters over. How's that?'

'That's O.K. with me,' said Shadgold. 'I'll give you a ring first thing in the morning, and we might have lunch together.'

'Then that's settled,' remarked the dramatist. 'In the meanwhile I'll re-read everything that's been printed about these murders, so that I've got the whole thing at my finger tips.'

Shadgold rose and held out his hand.

'Well, thank you very much, Mr. Lowe,' he said. 'I must be off now. I've got to get some sort of a meal before I leave.'

Trevor Lowe accompanied him to the door, and then returning to his study he searched among a file of newspapers and carried a number of them over to his desk. With a writing-block beside him he waded steadily through the papers, making an occasional note as he proceeded. It was eight o'clock when he finished, and got up and stretched himself with a yawn.

'Shadgold was right,' he muttered, as he poured himself out a drink. It's not going to be at all easy.'

Just how difficult it was really going to be the events of the next few days were to show him.

6

A Conference

Detective-Inspector Shadgold arrived in Hill Green shortly before nine and made straight for the police station in order to introduce himself to the local inspector with whom he was going to work.

He was conducted through the charge-room to a large and spacious office at the back, and to his surprise found not only Inspector Lightfoot waiting to receive him, but Major Payton, the chief constable, as well.

The reason for Payton's presence was because he expected a certain amount of constraint. He had over-ruled his subordinate in asking the aid of Scotland Yard, and he knew that Inspector Lightfoot was feeling a little sore at the case of his life being taken out of his hands. Therefore, Payton, who wanted to avoid as much friction as possible, when he learned by telephone that Shadgold was on his way down, decided to be present and, if necessary, pour oil on any troubled waters there might be.

He greeted Shadgold with a pleasant smile, and asked him if he would like any refreshment after his journey.

'No thank you, sir,' replied the red-faced inspector. 'I dined before I left London.'

'That's excellent,' said Payton. 'Then we can get to business at once. Let me introduce you to Inspector Lightfoot and Sergeant Bolton.'

Shadgold turned towards the two stiff figures seated at the table and tried to smile genially. It was difficult.

Inspector Lightfoot, red-haired and stern of eye, regarded him stonily. His face was hard and wooden, and, if he had any feelings, a mask for those feelings. Sergeant Bolton was thin and dark. A lugubrious, melancholy man whose blue, watery eyes looked reproachfully at this cuckoo that had invaded their nest.

Shadgold summoned up his courage.

'How d'you do?' he said. 'Pleased to meet you!'

He received in return a slight bow from Lightfoot and a grunt from Bolton. The chief constable, hastily stepping into the breach, pushed forward a chair.

'Sit down, Inspector,' he said cheerfully, 'and let's talk the thing over.'

Shadgold sat down on the right of the chief constable, and, facing the other two, waited. There was a silence. The chief constable moved uneasily in his chair and glanced at Inspector Lightfoot. Inspector Lightfoot glanced at the chief constable and cleared his throat. Shadgold had been in similar situations not once but many times, and he had his own methods. He thrust down his naturally truculent impulses and became as pleasant as possible. He smiled impartially at all three.

The chief constable coughed.

'I think it would be as well if Inspector Lightfoot gave you a detailed account of the case,' he said. 'I presume you know little or nothing about it at present?'

'I know nothing except what I have seen in the papers,' replied Shadgold. 'I shall be grateful if Inspector Lightfoot will let me have all details and also tell me how far he has got with his investigations.

The graciousness of his manner had its effect. The inspector visibly thawed. The hardness of his face softened. He felt in his pocket and produced a bulky notebook. Opening it, he laid it on the table in front of him, and began in an official voice to tell his story, refreshing his memory every now and again by consulting his notes.

Shadgold listened intently without making any comment. There was very little more than he had already seen in the newspapers. He gathered that everybody remotely connected with the deceased people had been interviewed and questioned, but without any very useful result. Boiled down to the bones what Inspector Lightfoot had to tell him was simply this: Two people within two days had been murdered by hanging, and there was absolutely no clue at all to the identity of the murderer.

'That's all,' said Lightfoot, closing his book with a snap. 'And precious little it is.'

'I don't see what more you could have

done, though, Inspector,' said Shadgold tactfully. 'It's a very difficult job — very difficult indeed.'

'It's an impossible job,' grunted Lightfoot, though he looked rather pleased at the Scotland Yard man's praise.

'What we have got to do is to make it possible,' said the chief constable. 'This unknown killer has got to be caught, and before he can do any further damage.'

Shadgold nodded thoughtfully.

'Have you any suggestions to make, sir?' he asked, respectfully. 'I mean, have you thought out any line of investigation you'd like us to follow?'

Major Payton rested his elbows on the table and leaned forward.

'I have, as a matter of fact, got a suggestion to make,' he admitted.

Inspector Lightfoot leaned back in his chair, and his attitude suggested that he was prepared for the worst. Sergeant Bolton yawned, hastily realized what he was doing, and converted the yawn into a sneeze. Shadgold, inwardly amused, regarded the chief constable with respectful interest.

'Both you, sir, and Inspector Lightfoot

are so much better acquainted with the neighbourhood and its residents than me,' he said, 'that I shall be very glad to hear what you suggest.'

Major Payton coughed.

'I'm afraid,' he began a little apologetically, 'that it isn't much of a suggestion, but it may prove helpful.' He looked from one to the other and then went on: 'I think we are all agreed that the possibility that these murders are the work of a lunatic is a very likely one.'

'It seems the only sensible solution,' grunted Lightfoot.

'Up to now,' amended Shadgold. 'Personally, I should like to exhaust all other explanations before definitely agreeing with that one.'

'Quite, quite!' said the chief constable hastily. 'But I think it's a possibility that must be borne in mind, and therefore my suggestion is this; that an inquiry should be started to try and discover all the persons of weak intellect in the vicinity of Hill Green, and, having done so, check up their movements at the times these two crimes were committed.'

Shadgold looked interested. This man was cleverer than he had expected.

'That's a very good idea, sir,' he said approvingly.

Major Payton looked pleased.

'What do you think, Inspector?' he asked, turning to Lightfoot.

Lightfoot nodded heavily.

'I like the scheme, sir,' he said, 'but it's going to be difficult to carry out. How are we going to find out who the barmy people are?'

'That shouldn't be very difficult,' said the Scotland Yard man. 'The doctors would probably be able to give you the information you require. No' — he shook his bullet head slowly — 'that won't be the difficulty. There are two objections to your idea, sir, if you don't mind my saying so.' He looked across at Major Payton.

'Not at all, not at all,' said the chief constable graciously. 'We are here to discuss the matter. Go on.'

'Well, then, sir,' said Shadgold, 'the objections are these: If these murders are the work of a homicidal maniac it's quite possible that neither the doctors nor anyone else would know that there was anything the matter with him. I mean that he would probably be normal in every way except for the killing streak. That's the first objection. The other is, supposing this isn't the work of a lunatic but somebody who, for his own ends, wants to make it appear that it is. What then?'

'Well, in the latter case,' answered Payton, 'our inquiry will have no result, except,' he added as a sudden thought occurred to him, 'it will make the killer think he has fooled us, and so give him a false sense of security, which might lead to his giving himself away.'

'Yes, there's something in that,' agreed the burly inspector. 'It's a very good kicking-off point, sir, anyway, and I think it should be tried.'

'I'll arrange to set some men at work first thing in the morning,' said Lightfoot.

'There's another line that I think should be followed up,' remarked Shadgold, and was secretly gratified to notice that the chilliness in the atmosphere was thawing fast. 'We should try and discover if there's anything in the lives of the two victims that connect them — apart, I mean, from the fact that they were distant cousins. A connection that might result in finding a common motive for somebody wanting these two out of the way.'

'On to that already,' growled Lightfoot. 'Expect to get the reports through on Monday or Tuesday.'

'Good!' approved the Scotland Yard man. 'Then at the moment that's all I've got to suggest. To-morrow I should like to have a look at the scenes of both the crimes.'

'I'll meet you here at any time you like,' said Lightfoot. 'How would ten o'clock suit you?'

Shadgold nodded.

'That'll suit me fine,' he said. 'And now I must go and see about some quarters, sir. I haven't fixed anywhere to stay yet.'

'We have arranged that for you,' said the chief constable. 'Sergeant Bolton has booked a room for you in the house where he lodges.'

'That's right,' mumbled the melancholy Sergeant Bolton.

Shadgold thanked the chief constable,

but inwardly he was not at all sure that he relished sharing the same roof with the lugubrious Bolton. He would infinitely have preferred a room in some quiet little inn on his own. However, the arrangements had been made, and he could not very well alter it without giving offence, and that was the last thing he wished to do.

The conference broke up soon after, and Major Payton departed homewards in his car, after extracting a promise that they would keep in touch with him regarding any discoveries that might be made. Shadgold said good night to Inspector Lightfoot, and was glad to find that individual a little more cordial than at their meeting. He went off with Bolton, and found that the sergeant lived quite close to the police station in one of a small row of cottages that faced some allotments.

His room was comfortable, and when he had arranged for his car to be garaged a tasty supper, flanked by a bottle of beer, was served to him by the rosy-faced woman to whom the cottage belonged.

Shadgold was tired, and it was not long before he was in bed, and snuggling his head into the lavender-scented pillow. But it was a long time before he was asleep. Over and over again he considered all the details of the case, and the more he thought of it the more difficult appeared the task that lay before him. The last thought that ran out of his brain as sleep took possession of it was one of thankfulness that Trevor Lowe would be coming down in the morning.

7

Lunch For Two

Sunday at Hill Green was neither a day of rest nor a day of toil. Providing it was reasonably fine, the golf course became a mass of colourful dots, which on closer inspection turned out to be a collection of the latest tweed suitings in many and varying designs. From midday on Saturday to seven o'clock on Monday morning the residents forgot such things as offices, banks, shops and the like where the greater part of their lives were spent, and became people of leisure. They played golf in the morning and bridge in the evening, and the more advanced among the community even went to the extent of throwing an occasional cocktail party.

On Sunday the insistent call of the 8.20 from Hill Green station was forgotten. Mr. Stott and his friend Mr. Julian Rusk, clad in rather startling plus-fours, the product of a tailor whom they both patronized in the City, sallied forth after a large and leisurely breakfast to the links, and there met other and equally brilliantly clad friends.

Mr. Rusk, who was staying with his friend while his wife was on a visit to a sick aunt, had during the last few days thoroughly enjoyed himself. He had found himself miraculously thrust into the limelight through no effort of his own, and innumerable drinks and invitations to lunch had been showered on him. Mr. Stott also had become quite a celebrity not only in Hill Green, but at his place of business. This, to them, pleasing state of affairs had been brought about merely by the fact that they had found the body of the unfortunate Doctor Wallington.

At the golf course they met an almost equally famous resident in the person of Mr. Cyril Haytor, who had been the last to see Miss Mortimer alive. He was not quite such a big noise as the others, for he had only seen Miss Mortimer before the murder, whereas they had discovered Doctor Wallington after — a small matter on which to base a degree of fame, but large in the eyes of the inhabitants of Hill Green.

'I understand,' said Mr. Stott, as he prepared to drive from the first tee, 'that the detective from Scotland Yard arrived last night.'

His opponents, Mr. Pifkin, the manager of Hill Green bank, and Mr. Widgerton, the secretary of the Hill Green Estate Company, looked interested.

'Indeed,' said Mr. Pifkin, puffing out his red, round and shining cheeks. 'Indeed!'

'I hope,' remarked Mr. Widgerton, 'that he will soon discover the author of these tragedies. This kind of thing isn't going to do the estate any good, you know.'

Mr. Stott, after carefully addressing his ball, drove it nearly a hundred yards down the fairway — a really excellent drive.

'No,' he agreed. 'It's the sort of publicity you don't want.'

'For my part,' said Mr. Pifkin, 'I think it's the work of a lunatic, and they are going to find it very difficult to catch him.'

'Oh, I don't know; these Scotland Yard

fellows are very smart, very smart indeed,' said Mr. Rusk, with an air of authority, as though he were personally acquainted with all of them. 'I think it's a very good thing that the local police have had the sense to ask for help.'

'It's a question of experience,' said Mr. Widgerton profoundly. 'Our men are quite smart; but they seldom come in contact with major crime, and, therefore, they can't be expected to deal with it so well.'

'That's right,' asserted Mr. Stott. 'Well, let's hope this London man will get busy.'

The London man was, as a matter of fact, getting very busy indeed.

He rose early, and after breakfast inquired the way to the nearest telephone. The nearest telephone, it appeared, was the police station; but there was another — a call-box at the junction of Hay Street and Meadow Lane. Shadgold chose the call-box, and fifteen minutes later was speaking to Trevor Lowe.

'Well, I'm here,' he said, 'and so far have learned very little more than what has been published in the newspapers. I'm going to meet Lightfoot — that's the local man — and have a look at the places where the bodies were found. That's really a matter of routine; I don't expect to learn anything much.'

'What a lot of wasted time routine has to answer for,' said Lowe's voice, and Shadgold could almost see the dramatist smiling. 'However, you never know. You might pick up something. I suppose you haven't seen the bodies yet?'

'No,' answered Shadgold.

'I should have a look at them as soon as possible, if I were you,' recommended Lowe. 'I'm inclined to think that you'll find them of more interest than the places where they were found.'

'How?' demanded the Scotland Yard man quickly.

'What's in your mind?'

'I'll tell you when I get down there,' said Lowe. 'I'm leaving here in about an hour, so I should be with you about twelve.'

'Where am I to meet you?' asked Shadgold.

There was a moment's silence before Lowe replied.

'Isn't there a sort of glorified pub near

the station?' he asked. 'There usually is in these places?'

'Yes, there is,' answered the stout inspector. He remembered passing it when he had arrived the previous night. 'It's the something hotel, I don't know the name.'

'I'll meet you there,' said Lowe. 'They can probably do something in the way of lunch, so we might as well have it together.'

Shadgold left the call-box and set off to keep his appointment with Lightfoot, feeling rather relieved. The responsibilities of this difficult case no longer rested entirely on his shoulders.

He arrived at the police station a few minutes early; but Inspector Lightfoot was already there, and greeted him pleasantly. Apparently his original antipathy to this interloper had become appreciably lessened.

'I think we had better go to Milton's Rise first, Inspector,' he said. 'Leeman's barn, where Miss Mortimer was found, lies farther on in the same direction.'

Shadgold agreed, and they set off. It

was a fair step from the police station to the Rise; but the morning was fine, and the Scotland Yard man enjoyed the walk. He chatted to Lightfoot about Hill Green and its residents; sympathized with the local man's lack of opportunities, and found that when you got to know him the inspector was quite a human and likeable person.

They came to the Rise at last, and Lightfoot pointed out the fatal lamp-post.

'That's where Doctor Wallington was found,' he said.

Shadgold looked at the post, and then at the roadway. Then he glanced at the rows of neat houses on either side.

'The murderer must have taken a big risk,' he remarked. 'At that hour of the evening there must have been quite a number of people who might have been looking out of any of their windows.'

Lightfoot agreed.

'Yes, you're right,' he nodded. 'But curiously enough nobody did see him. I've had house to house inquiries made, and nobody can give any information at all.'

Shadgold's eyes came back to the lamp-post.

'It must have taken some time, too,' he murmured thoughtfully. 'He had to tie the rope on to that iron bar and then slip the noose over his victim's head — it was an extraordinary risk to take.'

'The rope wasn't tied to the bar,' said Inspector Lightfoot. 'It had a loop made in it, and this had been slipped over the end of the bar. It's my opinion,' he added, 'that Doctor Wallington was unconscious before he was hanged.'

'He must have been,' said Shadgold, 'otherwise he would have made some sort of outcry and put up a struggle, and that would undoubtedly have been heard by somebody living in these houses.'

He looked around him again, and now became aware that they were being watched surreptitiously by the inhabitants of the houses adjacent to the spot.

There was a slight movement at several of the windows, and he caught sight of dim faces peering through the glass.

'There's certainly nothing much to be learned here,' he said after a careful scrutiny of the roadway. 'Perhaps we shall have better luck at the barn.'

'I doubt it,' remarked Lightfoot. 'I've been all over that barn with a fine-tooth comb, and there's nothing at all. However, you'd better see the place.'

They left Milton's Rise, followed by the curious eyes that had been watching them, and set off for Leeman's barn.

It was situated in the corner of a field, and backed by a small wood of thickly-growing trees. Here, thought Shadgold, a dozen murders might have been committed without risk of being overlooked, for there was not a habitation in sight. By the side of the barn was a five-barred gate that opened on to a narrow cart track, one end of which, Lightfoot explained, led to the farm and the other to the main road.

'You can't learn anything from that, though,' he concluded. 'So many carts pass up and down it that the surface doesn't hold any marks.'

They entered the barn. The padlock had not yet been repaired since it had been smashed by the killer of Miss Mortimer, and therefore they had no difficulty. It was a strongly-built place, and contained nothing beyond some heaps of straw and a few old boxes. From one end to the other ran a heavy beam, from which rose baulks of timber supporting the roof. It was from this beam that Miss Mortimer had been found hanging.

Shadgold made a careful inspection of the place, but at the end had to admit that there was nothing. Nor was there anything outside.

'Lunatic or otherwise,' he grunted at last, 'he's been deuced clever. There's not a trace.'

Lightfoot nodded in gloomy agreement.

'Two murders and not the ghost of a clue,' he said. 'No suspicion of motive, no nothing! Pleasant, ain't it?'

Shadgold thought it was anything but pleasant, and said so.

'Nothing to start on,' said Lightfoot. 'Nothing you can, so to speak, get your teeth in.'

'No, it's a pretty dead end,' replied the Scotland Yard man, frowning. 'By the way, when is the inquest?'

'Tuesday, at ten,' said Lightfoot. 'We

shall, of course, ask for an adjournment pending inquiries.'

They left the barn and began to make their way back to the police station.

'I should like to have a word with your divisional-surgeon,' said Shadgold, 'and also see the bodies.'

'Do that this afternoon,' answered Lightfoot. 'I'll telephone Doctor Murford to come along to the station at three.'

It was now getting on for twelve, and, leaving the local inspector at the station, Shadgold found his way to the 'glorified pub,' where he had arranged to meet Trevor Lowe.

He discovered that the place rejoiced in the name of the 'Hillside Hotel,' though why it had been called that nobody but the owners knew.

It was larger and more comfortable than he had expected, and he found that Lowe had already arrived and was waiting for him in the smoking-room. The dramatist had already booked a room and ordered lunch. He settled Shadgold in a comfortable chair, ordered sherries for both of them, and took his seat opposite the Scotland Yard man. There was nobody else in the smoking-room, so their conversation was unlikely to be overheard.

'Well?' he inquired when the drinks had been brought and the waiter had made himself scarce.

Shadgold sipped his sherry and shook his head.

'It's not well at all, Mr. Lowe,' he replied. 'I'll tell you what I've done so far — which isn't much.'

He gave a brief account of what had happened since his arrival.

'Which all amounts to absolutely nothing,' he concluded. 'And if you can suggest how I'm going to make a start on this business you're cleverer than I am.'

'On the face of it, it certainly looks a bit of a pill,' said the dramatist, frowning. 'That suggestion of the chief constable's is by no means a bad one.'

'No, it isn't,' said Shadgold. 'He's a nice fellow, too; nothing of the old Army officer.'

'H'm, you're going to see Doctor Murford this afternoon, you say?' asked Lowe, and Shadgold nodded. 'Well, I suggest,' the dramatist went on, 'that you question him as to the possibility of death having been caused by some other means than hanging.'

'Eh!' Shadgold opened his eyes wide and stared at his friend. 'What's the idea?'

'Well, it seems pretty obvious to me,' said the dramatist, 'that these two unfortunate people — particularly Doctor Wallington — must have been dead before they were hanged. The risk of hanging a live man to that lamp-post is too great for even a madman to take. But if Wallington was already dead with the rope round his neck and brought there in a car, the murderer had only to slip the loop over the iron rod — he could do this by lifting the body up to the required height — and clear off. It would take less than a minute, and would account for him not having been seen.'

'That's true,' admitted the inspector.

'Of course,' continued Lowe, 'he may have hanged them elsewhere; but I'm inclined to doubt if he would have done that. I think it's more likely than not that they were strangled with a scarf or cord, and then taken to the places where they were eventually found.'

'You may be right,' said the Scotland Yard man. 'But, even if you are, I don't see how it's going to help us find out the killer.'

'It at least gives you another line of investigation,' explained the dramatist. 'For instance, there may be something on the bodies that will give you a clue to the place where they were actually killed, and if you can find that you're a good step further on.'

Shadgold looked a little dubious.

'A very small step,' he grunted.

'That,' disagreed Lowe, 'you can't possibly say. For all you know the place might be a house in the district. If you can prove that it was, then a very strong suspicion would rest on the person, or persons, to whom the house belonged, or who lived in it.'

'H'm,' said the other. 'It sounds all right, but it's only a theory that these crimes were committed elsewhere. We have no proof.'

Trevor Lowe shrugged his shoulders.

'We've no proof of anything,' he said.

'Except that two people have been killed by somebody unknown. What we've got to do is to turn that 'somebody unknown' into somebody known, and unless another murder is committed, and the killer gives himself away, we can only do it by following up every possible thread, however thin.'

Shadgold nodded in reluctant agreement.

Although he did not know it then, he already held in his hands one end of a thread that was eventually to lead him to the truth.

8

Two Who Feared

There was a portion of Hill Green called the Square. It was a considerably older portion than the rest of the Garden City, and was not under the jurisdiction of the Hill Green Estate Company, although they had tried their best to acquire it.

The houses of the Square, though by no means ancient, were antiques compared with the stucco and brick of Hill Green proper. They were grouped picturesquely about a central garden, in which the inhabitants could play tennis all the year round, if they were so disposed, on the four hard courts that had been built for that purpose. The garden was beautifully kept, and enclosed by iron railings, in which were set two gates, and only the fortunate people who lived in the Square had a key or were permitted to enter.

These superior beings rather looked down on the rest of Hill Green. They regarded themselves much in the light of feudal lords, and considered the rest of the community little better than peasants. None of them was ever seen upon the golf course; those that played that energetic game were members of the Royal Langham Club, three miles away. The much used — and much abused — 8.20 never carried any of them on its daily journey to London. If they had occasion to travel, they travelled discreetly in their own cars.

The Hill Green residents said nasty things about them, sneered at their airs and graces, and secretly envied them.

Joyce Elliot was not quite so bad as her neighbours but constant association with them had made her inclined to wear a rather haughty air which her enemies described as supercilious, but which was really nothing of the sort. She had lived in the Square all her life — at least, as much of her life as she could remember; had torn round the beautifully kept gravel paths of the garden on a scooter, all legs and hair; had outgrown short frocks and plaited tresses and suddenly developed into a very pretty girl. There were people who would have disagreed in this latter description, but they were all of her own sex, and their criticism was prompted by envy. At twenty-two, Joyce Elliot was tall and slim, with a complexion that owed nothing to artifice but was purely a product of Nature. Her brown hair, which in the sunlight gleamed with splashes of gold, matched the eyes, large and widely set. She was not beautiful, her features were too irregular, but looking at her you felt completely satisfied, which is probably a greater tribute to her charm.

She was an orphan, and lived with her dead mother's brother in the low, half-timbered house that was the only home she could remember.

Mr. Nethcott — whom she always referred to as 'Pops' — had been both father and mother to the parentless child, and until the arrival of his brother she had been completely happy and carefree. But with Harold Nethcott's inclusion in the establishment a shadow had slowly deepened until it had reached appalling aspects. The change had first been apparent in Mr. Nethcott. He had grown more and more careworn and worried, and sometimes, when she had been reading, and he thought that nobody was watching him, she had seen an expression come into his eyes that could only be described as haunted. He had made evasive replies to all her efforts to find out what the trouble was, and now the climax had been reached. For the last three days he had been a broken man, a mere ghost of his former robust and laughing self.

Standing by the window of the long drawing-room and looking out into the peace of that Sunday afternoon, Joyce wondered that he did not look worse than he did, for on the previous night she had learnt for the first time the reason for that shadow which had come to the house.

A sleepless night had done nothing to dissipate the first horrible shock of her discovery. Even now it scarcely seemed that the dreadful thing Pops had told her could be true. It was nightmarish — terrible.

She turned away from the window as the door opened and Francis Nethcott came in. He was a dapper little man with grey hair that was rapidly thinning on the top. His pleasant face was drawn and haggard, and the skin hung loosely about his mouth and on his neck.

'Where is Uncle Harold?' she asked in a low voice.

He came towards her, thrusting his hands into his trousers' pockets with a curious little nervous gesture.

'Sleeping,' he said briefly. 'He's quite normal.'

He walked over to the mantelpiece and touched an ornament, setting it straight with elaborate care.

'We must keep the papers away from him,' he continued. 'We mustn't risk another — shock.'

Joyce looked at him, and her eyes were full of sympathy.

'Isn't it — dreadful?' she murmured.

He turned and faced her.

'It may not be so bad as we think,' he answered. 'That account of the — the — murders may have only — touched some chord in his memory. It may not be any worse than that.'

'He was out late on Saturday night,' she said, steadily. 'I heard him come in.'

'You're sure it was — Harold — not one of the servants?' he asked.

'I'm sure,' she answered. 'I was awake, and I heard his steps coming upstairs. I wondered who it could be at that hour, and I opened my door. I saw Uncle Harold just going into his room.'

He made a gesture of despair.

'The terrible thing is that I don't know what to do,' he said huskily. 'I know what I ought to do. What it is my duty to do, but I — can't.'

She came over to him and put her hand on his shoulder.

'Poor Pops,' she said softly. 'I'm terribly sorry.'

He patted her hand gently.

'It's as bad for you — almost, my dear,' he said. 'It's a dreadful responsibility for both of us.'

For a moment there was a silence, which Joyce broke.

'I suppose — he hasn't — said

anything?' she asked.

The little man shook his head.

'No, no, not a word. After that outburst on — on Friday he's been just his usual self.' He sighed heavily. 'If he's in any way responsible, I'll swear he doesn't know it.'

'He mustn't be allowed to go out by himself,' said the girl decidedly. 'You must see to that, Pops.'

'Oh, I shall, my dear,' said Francis Nethcott.

'The danger is,' went on the girl quickly, 'if anybody should suspect — the police — '

'That's what's worrying me,' admitted the little man. 'But I don't see how they can. I changed my name to Nethcott when the first trouble came, and that was before I came to live here when you were quite a baby. When I brought Harold back — last year — he adopted the name of Nethcott, too.'

Joyce frowned. Since the previous night she seemed to have aged appreciably.

'But surely he must remember — all that — ' She broke off and shivered.

'He doesn't remember anything,' declared

Nethcott. 'Even the report in the newspapers didn't have the effect of awakening his memory. It upset him, but he couldn't say why. Thank God he doesn't remember,' he added vehemently.

'What about the servants,' said Joyce. 'Supposing they talk — '

'The only one who knows the truth is Lane,' answered Nethcott, 'and he won't talk.'

The girl smiled — a rather anæmic attempt, but still a smile. Lane, the silver-haired old butler, was a particular favourite of hers.

'No, Lane is safe enough,' she agreed. 'So long as the police don't trace any connection we are all safe — '

There came a gentle tap at the door, and in answer to Nethcott's invitation, a maid entered.

'What is it, Ann?' asked the girl.

'If you please, Miss,' answered the servant, 'Mr. Bryant has called.'

'Oh, yes, ask him to come in,' said Joyce; and then, as the maid withdrew: 'I'd forgotten Jim was coming. I've promised to go for a walk with him this afternoon.'

Nethcott nodded.

'It'll do you good, my dear,' he said and going to the girl he squeezed her arm. 'Don't let yourself worry too much.'

He looked round as a young man came in unannounced.

'Hullo, Joyce, I think I'm a bit early,' he greeted. 'Good afternoon, sir.'

'Afternoon, Jim,' said Nethcott. 'How's your father? That spasm any better?'

'Pretty nearly all right now,' replied Bryant. 'I expect he'll be about again in a few days. You're not looking too well, though, sir.'

Nethcott laughed, a rather mirthless sound.

'I feel fairly all right,' he said. 'Slight touch of indigestion but nothing serious.'

'I'll go and put my things on,' said Joyce. 'I won't keep you a minute, Jim.'

'Right-ho!' He smiled, and she went quickly out.

Jim had known Joyce Nethcott since she was a small child. They had played together and grown up together — and — so said the people of the Square — fallen in love together, though no word of this had ever been mentioned between themselves. They were, however, inseparable friends, and were nearly always in each other's company. The elder Bryant, a widower, was a great friend of Francis Nethcott's, and the possibility of Joyce and Jim eventually marrying and settling down had often been discussed between them.

Nethcott thought of this as he looked at the pleasant-faced boy before him, and sighed. What would be the attitude of his old friend if he knew the truth?

'Have you heard the latest news about these murders, sir?' said Jim, and the little man started.

'No,' he stammered. 'What — what is it?'

'It's all over the place,' answered Jim. 'I heard it from the Vennings. Trevor Lowe's come down.'

Nethcott gripped the back of a chair, and his grey face went ashen.

'Came down this morning,' Jim continued, smiling pleasantly. 'At least that's what they say. I don't know whether it's true or not. He's rather good at this sort of thing. Does it for a hobby in between writing plays, and I should think he might be pretty useful in getting this business cleared up. Why, what's the matter, sir?' His voice changed to a note of concern, and he sprang forward as the little man swayed.

'It's nothing — nothing, my boy,' croaked Nethcott quickly, and made a violent effort to recover himself. 'Rather a sudden pain from that indigestion I was talking about.'

'You ought to see a doctor, sir,' said Jim. 'By Jove, you look pretty bad!'

'I'm all right, quite all right,' he had gained control of his voice, but the perspiration stood out in little beads on his forehead. 'Yes, perhaps I will see a doctor — ' He broke off as Joyce came in, ready for her walk. 'Off you go, you two,' he said lightly. 'Don't make her late for tea, Jim.'

Going to the window, he watched them leave the house, and then with unsteady steps came back to the settee. With almost a groan he sank down on the soft cushions and buried his face in his hands.

Another one had been added to the people who were looking for the Hill Green murderer. And the man they were searching for, the man who signed himself 'The Hangman,' was at that moment, so Nethcott believed, in the room above sleeping as peacefully as a child.

9

The Nail

The news of Trevor Lowe's presence in Hill Green spread with the rapidity of an epidemic. The booking clerk at the 'Hillside Hotel' mentioned it to the porter, and the porter told the barman. Before Shadgold and the dramatist had finished their lunch it was half way round the community.

After they had had coffee in the smoking-room they went down to the police station, and Lowe was introduced to Inspector Lightfoot. This needed rather careful handling, for the dramatist's reputation was well known since the publicity afforded by the affair at Phantom Hollow. But Shadgold rose nobly to the occasion. After Lowe and the inspector had shaken hands, the Scotland Yard man drew Lightfoot to one side.

'Mr. Lowe and I are old friends,

Inspector,' he said, 'and I thought he might be very useful to us in this business. Having no official capacity, we need have no fear of his stealing our thunder in any way.'

Lightfoot nodded rather grudgingly.

'It's your business Mr. Shadgold,' he said. 'You're in charge of this case now, not me.'

'That's all nonsense!' remonstrated the stout inspector. 'We're acting together. I shouldn't dream of doing anything without your consent.'

Lightfoot was a little mollified, but still rather obviously resented Lowe's presence. The dramatist quickly saw how the land lay, and during the ensuing quarter of an hour while they chatted over the business that had brought them together, he laid himself out to remove the slight feeling of constraint that existed. There were few people who could resist his charm of manner when he chose to exert himself, and certainly Inspector Lightfoot was not one of them. When they left the station to go to the mortuary he had entirely capitulated.

The mortuary at Hill Green was a converted shed, in the charge of a very young and very rural policeman. It was a gloomy building, lighted by one small window high up near the roof. In consequence, the interior was in a state of semi-twilight. Side by side against the wall were two trestle tables, their contents covered by white sheets.

'We have no proper mortuary at Hill Green,' explained Inspector Lightfoot unnecessarily, 'so we had to make shift as best we could with this.' He turned to the gaping policeman. 'Light the lamp, Rogers,' he ordered.

Rogers took down from a shelf a powerful incandescent oil lamp, fiddled about with it for a moment or two, and then applied a match to the mantle. A pitiless white glare lit up the shed.

'Now, Mr. Shadgold,' said Lightfoot, 'if you want to look at the bodies you'll be able to see what you're about.'

Shadgold thanked him, and together with Lowe approached the first of the trestle tables. Gently he pulled back the sheet, and bent over the thing that lay beneath. In spite of the fact that he was used to such sights, he had to repress a shudder as he looked at what had once been Doctor Wallington.

'God, how horrible!' he said below his breath.

'Not very pleasant, is it?' muttered Lowe, and steeling himself against his natural repugnance, he bent closer to look at the throat.

The mark where the rope had gone was still visible, a blue-black circle on the purple flesh, but it was impossible to come to any conclusion as to whether death had actually been the result of the hanging, or had taken place before. Shadgold gently replaced the sheet, and they turned to the other table. Here the result was practically the same. Both the victims of the unknown killer could quite easily have been dead before they had been hanged, provided death had been brought about by some form of strangulation. Lowe whispered something to Shadgold and he nodded. Straightening up, he turned to Inspector Lightfoot.

'Have you got the clothing?' he asked.

'Yes,' said Lightfoot, and went over to a box that stood in one corner.

Taking a key from his pocket he unlocked it, and came back with his arms full of clothes.

'There you are,' he said, putting them down on a plain wooden table. 'I don't think you'll get much from them, though. I've been over every inch of them.'

Shadgold said nothing, but sorting out the various articles, he submitted them to a perfunctory scrutiny, and then passed them on to Lowe, who looked at them a little more closely.

Irene Mortimer had apparently been wearing a cloth coat trimmed with fur, and at the collar of this the dramatist stared intently.

'What have you found, Mr. Lowe?' asked the Scotland Yard man quickly.

Lowe extracted something that was caught up among the fur, and put it in the palm of his hand. Peering over his shoulder, Shadgold and Lightfoot gazed at the tiny object interestedly. It was a ragged portion of finger-nail, jagged and uneven.

'By Jove!' breathed the red-faced inspector excitedly. 'That's something, anyway.'

'It must have been ripped off during some sort of a struggle,' murmured the dramatist. 'As you say, it's something and it tells us two things.' He turned the little scrap over with his finger.

'Two things?' repeated Lightfoot inquiringly.

Lowe nodded.

'Yes,' he replied. 'It tells us that the person we have to look for is a man — this obviously never came from a woman's hand — and that he is probably fairly well off, and to be found among the middle or upper classes. It tells us a third thing, too, but that is so obvious that I needn't mention it.'

'How do you get the second thing?' asked Lightfoot, frowning.

'The nail has come from a hand that has been regularly and carefully manicured,' explained the dramatist.

'What about the third point?' said Shadgold, and Lowe smiled.

'The third point is simply that you have to look for a man minus half a nail on one of his fingers,' he replied, 'and that's going to narrow things down considerably.'

'I should say it is!' exclaimed Lightfoot excitedly, and then with a sudden contraction of his red eyebrows: 'I don't know how I came to miss it.'

'It was probably buried deep in the fur when you looked,' said Lowe. 'And later, perhaps in putting the things in that box, became shaken loose.' He handed it over to Shadgold. 'You'd better take care of it,' he said, 'it's going to be an important piece of evidence. Now, let's see if there's anything else.'

They continued their search of the clothing, but found nothing more.

'Is it possible to have a word with your divisional-surgeon?' asked Lowe, when Inspector Lightfoot had replaced the things in the box and locked it.

The inspector nodded.

'I asked him to come down to the station,' he replied. 'We'll probably find him waiting when we get back.'

They did find him, an impatient, fussy little man, who was not best pleased at being dragged out on a Sunday afternoon from the bosom of his family.

'Couldn't you have waited till Monday?' he grunted irritably. 'You've got my statement properly written out and signed. What more do you want?'

'This gentleman would like a little chat with you, Doctor,' said Inspector Lightfoot soothingly.

The little man swung round on Lowe.

'And who may you be, sir?' he snapped testily.

The inspector hastily introduced the dramatist.

'I've heard of you, of course,' grunted Doctor Murford, 'but I can't see why you want to talk to me.'

Lowe was tempted to reply that if he was always as disagreeable as this he could not see why anybody *ever* wanted to talk to him, but he tactfully refrained.

'It's just a question as to the cause of death, Doctor,' he began pleasantly, but the other interrupted him.

'Cause of death?' he snapped. 'Good God, isn't that obvious enough! What do you think killed 'em?'

'I'm waiting for you to tell us,' answered the dramatist quietly.

'Oh, I see,' the doctor's thin lips curled into a slight sneer. 'Well then, death was caused in both cases by asphyxiation due to hanging.'

'You are sure of that?' persisted Lowe, and the divisional-surgeon glared.

'Sure?' he exclaimed angrily. 'Of course I'm sure, man! What are you driving at? Do you think they were shot?'

By a great effort the dramatist kept his temper.

'No,' he said, 'but what I'm driving at is this. Could they have been killed by strangulation first and afterwards hanged?'

'I should think it very unlikely,' began Doctor Murford irritably, but Shadgold cut him short.

'However unlikely you may consider it, Doctor,' he said gently, 'doesn't concern the question. What we want to know is whether it could have happened.'

'Of course it could have happened,' admitted the doctor ungraciously. 'But it's impossible to say with any certainty whether it did or not. There are no other marks on the bodies, except those caused by the rope.'

The shrill ringing of the telephone bell broke in on the end of his sentence. Lightfoot answered the call.

'Oh, is that you, sir?' he said respectfully, and after a slight pause: 'Yes, it's quite true, sir, as a matter of fact he's here now. Would you like to speak to him?' With the receiver in his hand he turned to the dramatist. 'Major Payton, the chief constable, has heard that you are down here, Mr. Lowe,' he said. 'He'd like to speak to you.'

Lowe went over and took the black cylinder from his hand.

'Hullo!' he called into the mouthpiece.

'Is that Mr. Lowe?' a crisp voice came over the wire. 'Payton this end. I've just heard that you are at Hill Green and taking an interest in our murders.'

'I'm helping my friend, Inspector Shadgold, if that's what you mean,' replied Lowe.

'I don't mind who you're helping so long as you're here!' the voice chuckled. 'Perhaps if you're not doing anything better this evening you'd come along and dine with me, eh?'

'That's very nice of you,' answered the dramatist. 'I should be delighted.'

'Good!' said the chief constable. 'You're staying at the 'Hillside,' aren't you?'

'I am,' Lowe smiled. 'Have they told you what I had for lunch?' The other chuckled.

'Not quite as bad as that,' he said, 'but you must remember that ours is a small community. News travels fast, and you're rather a celebrity, you know. I'll send my car for you at seven-thirty. Don't bother to dress. I'm a bachelor myself, and I prefer to eat in comfort.'

'I'll be ready at seven-thirty,' said Lowe.

'Good,' said Payton again, and then: 'I suppose you haven't got hold of anything yet? But of course you haven't.'

'As a matter of fact we have,' answered the dramatist, slightly stressing the 'we,' and briefly told the interested man at the other end of the wire of the discovery of the finger-nail.

'I say, that's excellent,' said Payton when he had finished. 'That's going to be an immense help. Well then, I'll see you to-night.'

He rang off and Lowe hung up the receiver.

'If you don't want me any more,' said Doctor Murford, 'I'll be getting back home. Perhaps I can spend the rest of the afternoon without being disturbed.'

'I don't think we need detain you any longer,' said Shadgold, and with a curt nod the doctor left the station.

'Rather a surly fellow, isn't he?' remarked the Scotland Yard man.

'He's always like that,' said Lightfoot. 'It's more bark than bite, though. He suffers rather badly from migraine.'

'What's that?' asked Shadgold.

'Sort of extra bad headache,' explained Lightfoot. 'He gets an attack every now and again. As a matter of fact he's only just got over the last one. They always leave him in a bad temper.'

'What *I* should like to know,' remarked Lowe thoughtfully, 'is how he came to injure his left hand.'

'Eh, what's that, Mr. Lowe?' demanded Shadgold quickly.

'Didn't you notice?' asked the dramatist. 'He tried to hide it but the second finger of his left hand was covered by a finger-stall.'

They both stared at him in silence.

10

'Monkey' George

The weather broke at twelve o'clock on that Sunday night, and the rain came down in torrents. It hissed and splashed with almost tropical violence, and made every gutter a miniature cataract. At one o'clock the fields and lanes surrounding Hill Green were wastes of liquid mud. The trees and hedges masses of dripping foliage.

Mr. George Tidd looked out of the tiny kitchen window of his equally tiny cottage, and his habitual scowl deepened. Mr. Tidd was not a prepossessing individual. His face was cast in the Simian mould, with coarse black hair that grew low down on his narrow forehead. To the farmers and traders of the district he was known as 'Monkey' George, not so much on account of his appearance, as because of his reputation for petty pilfering. He had, in fact, twice been up before the bench, once on a charge of stealing agricultural implements, and once for poaching. Poaching was, in fact, Mr. Tidd's strong suit, and most nights found him prowling round the woods and coverts, his pockets full of snares, carrying on his livelihood. It was during one of these excursions that he had stumbled on his great adventure. His small eyes glistened in the light of the cheap oil lamp that illumined his abode, as he turned away from the window and came over to the fire-place. That accidental piece of luck was going to put a fortune in his pocket — easy money which would put unlimited beer within his reach. Mr. Tidd liked both beer and money so long as neither had to be obtained by work. Work was one of the things that in 'Monkey' George's eyes constituted the greater part of the seven deadly sins. 'Thou shalt not work' was to him an eleventh commandment which he did his best to break as seldom as possible. How he lived and managed to pay even the small rent demanded for his tumble-down cottage on the fringe of Leeman's wood was a mystery to the majority of Hill Green. It was, however, no mystery to Mr. Tidd, nor to certain unscrupulous shopkeepers in the neighbouring districts who purchased from him at bargain prices the results of his midnight prowling and asked no questions. This amazing piece of luck which had come his way would alter all that; in future he would be able to live in comfort, without having to dodge keepers and other unpleasant people who so consistently tried to rob him of his living. Before the sun rose he expected to be in possession of five hundred pounds, and he rubbed his dirty hands, and licked his thick lips in joy at the prospect. For Mr. Tidd held in his small and cunning brain the secret of the hanging murders, and had decided to exploit it to his own financial benefit. Attending to his illegal profession on the Friday night, he had been an unseen witness of the murder of Irene Mortimer, and the identity of 'The Hangman' was no mystery to him. His first inclination had been to go to the police, and then this greater and more pretentious scheme had suggested itself, with its prospects of unlimited wealth. He had thought it over slowly and with care, his limited intelligence awed by the magnitude of the prospect, and that afternoon had seen the budding of his plans. The result of his telephone call, couched in guarded language, had sent him home jubilant with the knowledge that the night would see the bud blossom into full flower. He glanced at the cheap tin clock on his mantelpiece. A quarter past one. In fifteen minutes it would be time to make a start to keep his appointment. He poured himself out another glass of beer from the bottle on the table, and drank it noisily and at a draught. Setting down the glass and wiping his mouth on the back of his hand, he took a packet of limp cigarettes from his waistcoat pocket and lit one. Life was very pleasant at that moment to 'Monkey' George; the future a dream seen through the rosy glasses of continuous affluence. He went over again to the window and looked out. The night was very black, and the rain still falling heavily. He cursed softly. He had a long way to go, and five minutes in that downpour would soak him to the skin. However, it had its advantages perhaps, for there would certainly be nobody else abroad to see his meeting with the man who represented the practical side to his dream of wealth. He began to struggle into his ragged overcoat, buttoning it tightly about his thick-set figure. He might as well go now and give himself plenty of time. The short cut across the field would be impossible to-night; he would have to take the longer way round by the road. But he had allowed for this in fixing his time for starting. He pulled on his cap, blew out the lamp, and opened the door of the cottage. The rain lashed his face as he shut the door behind him and set off into the wet darkness of the night. The junction at the four cross roads, which was his objective, was nearly a mile and a half away, but he would be able to do it easily. He stumbled along the rutted lane that wound round the edge of the wood, and presently came out upon a secondary road. It was easier walking here, though the darkness was so great that he could scarcely see more than two or three yards ahead. He hummed a tuneless dirge below his breath as he stumbled along, scraps of songs that he had heard on the wireless at the 'Load of Hay,' although nobody but he would have recognized any of them. It was, as near as he could judge, getting on for two o'clock when he reached the end of his journey, a rain-swept, deserted place where another road bisected the one by which he had come. Slowing down a little, he looked keenly about him. There was no sign of any living thing near. 'Monkey' George grunted. Of course, it was barely time, he was early, but supposing the bloke didn't come? Perhaps the rain would stop him? A moment's thought convinced him that this was unlikely. He'd come right enough. His life depended on his keeping the appointment. He, George Tidd, was a person to be treated with respect. One word from him to the police — his eyes narrowed. Away in the distance two dim star points of light were approaching. He watched them as they came nearer, drawing wider apart. Was this the man he was expecting or somebody who was out late? He drew back into the shadow of a dripping hedge. If the car stopped he would

101

be sure. He could hear the hiss of the tyres on the wet surface of the road now, and the faint rhythmic throbbing of the engine . . . A long, low blot of darkness, the car slid past him, slowed and — stopped! 'Monkey' George came out from the shelter of the overhanging hedge, and approached it. At the sound of his footsteps a head was thrust out of the near side window.

'Is that you, Tidd?' whispered the solitary occupant, and Mr. Tidd grunted.

''Corse it's me,' he growled. 'Do you think anyone else 'ud be at this adjectival place as late as this?'

He waited, expecting some reply, but none was made.

'Well,' he said impatiently, ''ave yer brought the dough?'

This time he got an answer.

'I have,' came the same low whisper.

''And it over then,' said 'Monkey' George, stretching out his hand, 'an' let me get back 'ome out of this perishin' rain.'

'Not so fast,' said the man in the car. 'How am I to know that you'll keep your mouth shut, after I've given you the money?'

'You'll 'ave to risk that,' replied Mr. Tidd with a grin. 'You've just got to take my word for it. But you can bet yer life if you don't 'and over that money, I shall open me mouth darned wide!'

There was another silence and it continued for so long that 'Monkey' George got impatient.

''Ere, don't go ter sleep!' he snarled. 'I don't want to stop 'ere all the blasted night.'

There was a click and the door of the car swung open. The occupant got out. For a moment he stood surveying the other, and then from the breast pocket of his heavy overcoat he took a packet.

'When I have given you this money,' he said softly, 'you must clearly understand that it will be the last. There will be no more.'

Mr. Tidd grinned evilly.

'We'll see about that later,' he growled. 'I dessay that'll do fer a bit, anyway. 'Ow much 'ave you got there?'

'The amount you asked for,' said the other. 'Five hundred pounds.'

'Monkey' George's little eyes glistened

with greed. Five hundred quid! All the money in the world — and his! He stretched out his hand eagerly.

'Give it me,' he whispered hoarsely.

The man in the heavy coat held out the packet. 'Monkey' George snatched it, and as he did so the man's other hand came from behind his back and gripped his wrist. A quick jerk and the poacher fell forward on his knees with a little gasping cry of fear. It was the last sound he ever uttered. Something soft was slipped round his neck and drawn tight, choking the scream that was forming in his throat. Tighter and tighter it drew until his lungs were bursting, and his heart was thumping madly . . . His head felt as if it were swelling to an enormous size, and his eyes began to start from their sockets . . . The blackness of the night turned red, a mottled red shot with huge flashes of orange flame . . . A roar like the rushing of a mighty torrent filled his ears, and then suddenly silence. Silence and blackness.

The murderer rose panting, and wiped his face. Quickly he glanced about him, and then picking up the dead man and kicking aside the packet — it only contained sheets of newspaper — carried him to the car. Unceremoniously he bundled the limp body into the back and took his place behind the wheel. The car jerked forward, gathered speed, and the red tail lamp faded into the mist of the rain-swept night . . .

11

The Third Crime

Trevor Lowe spent a very pleasant evening with the chief constable. Major Payton was a well-read man, and his conversation was interesting and sometimes brilliant. They discussed the drama, art, music and came by easy stages to criminology. He was obviously delighted that Lowe had come to Hill Green, and expressed a hope that the dramatist would succeed in helping to find a solution to the problem that was worrying them.

'For until this fellow, whoever he is, is run to earth,' he said, 'the whole community will be in a state of terror.'

They discussed the matter in detail, and it was with a feeling of real regret that Lowe took his leave shortly after ten o'clock. He elected to walk home to the 'Hillside Hotel,' for although the night was dark and cloudy, the rain had not yet started. He had much to occupy his mind, for apart from his anxiety to help Shadgold, the case interested him to a marked degree. It appealed strongly to his imagination, and to that sense of the dramatic which was naturally, considering his profession, such a large portion of his make-up. The methods of the unknown killer were so unusual. He tried to recollect from the accounts he had read of past crimes a case that was at all similar, and he found it difficult. Hanging as a means of murder was rare. There was the isolated case of Peter Bargoyne who hanged his father-in-law and tried to make it appear like suicide, and there was the other case of that fellow — what was his name — who had hanged his wife and little daughter. That was an old case, nineteen or twenty years old at the least. The man — what *was* his name — had been found insane and been sent to Widemoore. Smedley, that was the name! It suddenly came to him. Harold Smedley. These two cases were the only two that Lowe could remember, and even they were not quite like this one. Either the man who signed himself 'The Hangman' was stark, staring crazy, and killed for the mere pleasure of killing, or there was some very deep and subtle plot behind the whole thing. Now which was it? Lowe was a trifle reluctant to accept the homicidal maniac theory without more definite proof, and yet the alternative was even more difficult to believe. For if the murders were not the outcome of a madman's distorted brain, where was the motive?

Walking along through the silent streets he tried to imagine some plausible motive that would fit the facts. There were roughly three basic motives for murder. Gain, jealousy and revenge. These, of course, could be split up into varying groups under each main heading. There was a fourth motive, self-preservation, but it was less common than the other three. Under which heading — supposing the crimes were not the work of a lunatic — could he place a possible motive? Mentally he took them in order. Gain. This was the most common of all motives, but how did it come into this case? Apparently neither Doctor Wallington nor Miss Mortimer had been well off. Of course, as yet the inquiry into their personal affairs had not progressed far enough to be sure of this. Quite a large sum might be involved, and if this should turn out to be the case, then the next step would be to find out who benefited by their deaths. It was worth looking into, but Lowe was rather sceptical that it would prove to be as easy as this. The next possible motive was jealousy. Here again, as yet there was not sufficient data. Doctor Wallington and Miss Mortimer had been cousins, and there was the possibility that they might have been contemplating marriage and so aroused the jealousy of a third party. But this was merely a vague supposition unsupported by any tangible evidence. Revenge, the third motive on his list, Lowe had to treat in the same way. It presupposed that these two people had been instrumental in so injuring, directly or indirectly, another person that only their joint deaths could wipe out the wrong. The dramatist decided that this was rather far-fetched, and that brought him to the fourth and last category, self-preservation. Had Wallington and Miss Mortimer known something between them about a third person that rendered it absolutely necessary for them to be killed to preserve that person's safety. This was by no means impossible. It was, when he came to consider it, the most possible of the lot. If they had been in possession of such a secret, it must have been a very serious one. Of such magnitude as to warrant the risk of murder to preserve it. Perhaps when the police inquiries into their past lives had been completed, something of this nature would come to light. In the meanwhile, Lowe was back where he had begun. The stumbling block to all his hypotheses was lack of sufficient data. The pencilled message found pinned to each of the victims, why that? Why 'The Hangman'? Was it just the result of a disordered brain, or a gesture to try and make the crimes look like the work of a maniac. He had found no satisfactory answer to any of these questions by the time he reached the hotel. As he entered the rain began to fall, and he congratulated himself on having just missed a wetting.

He went straight up to his room, a large bedroom in the front of the house, with many windows that overlooked the street, and after smoking a cigarette, undressed and got into bed. But for some reason he found sleep difficult. Perhaps it was the lashing of the rain on the windows, or perhaps it was his own disjointed thoughts. Whatever it was, he kept twisting and turning restlessly, and it was some time before he dropped off into a troubled doze.

He awoke early, a glance at his watch showed him that it was barely six, and getting up, looked out at the morning. The rain had stopped, and by the look of things the day was going to be a fine one. In spite of his troubled night, he felt very wakeful, and decided to remain up. He rang the bell, and to a surprised and yawning chambermaid gave the order for his bath and breakfast. When he had dressed and finished the breakfast that was brought him, he lit a cigarette and opening the centre window, leaned out, resting his arms on the sill. The morning air was fresh and sweet, and he drew in deep breaths of nature's best tonic. The countryside looked very peaceful and still. A pale sun was just beginning to make its presence known, gilding the roof of the station with primrose light. He heard the measured tread of somebody approaching, and craning his neck to see who it was who was so early abroad, saw the blue-clad form of a policeman. He went by with the same unhurried tread, and his footsteps faded in the distance. Lowe smoked thoughtfully. The world — or rather that small part of it which lay within the range of his eyes and ears — was beginning to wake up. There came the rattle of a milk barrow, and the clang and hiss of a shunting engine. A paper-boy made his appearance, delivering the early newspapers. And then by ones and twos people began to make their way towards the station. Not the black-clad business population of Hill Green, but the earlier workers bent on catching the workman's train which would be due in three minutes. These people came not from Hill Green proper — nobody in Hill Green worked, they went to business — but from the less aristocratic part which lay in the vicinity of the railway. Lowe watched them vanishing into the station like industrious ants. He heard the train come in with a great deal of noise and puffing, and he heard it go out again with a great deal more. Presently he crushed out the end of his cigarette on the sill, and stretched out his hand to close the window, but he did not close it. A sound came to his ears, the sound of running steps, hurrying, stumbling footsteps. He leaned out, looking in the direction from which the sound came. A man was coming down the road, a man who was running with little jerky steps, as though he was almost spent.

Shadgold!

Lowe recognized the stout figure and red face of the Scotland Yard man. Nearer he came, and now the dramatist could hear the laboured gasping of his breath. At the entrance to the hotel he stopped, and tugged at the bell. Lowe drew in his head sharply, and strode across to the door. He was half way down the stairs when he heard Shadgold's voice demanding to see him, and a second later met the stout inspector in the lounge.

'Thank the Lord you're up, Mr. Lowe,' panted Shadgold. 'I was — afraid I'd have to wait — until you'd dressed . . . '

'What is it? What's happened?' asked Lowe, although he guessed the answer.

'Another of 'em!' breathed the Scotland Yard man, 'found hanging — in the Square this morning!'

12

Tar

There was a gardener provided by the local council whose duty it was to see that the enclosed space on which the houses of the Square looked out was kept in a condition suitable to the refined views of the residents. He began work at six in the summer, and eight in the winter, leaving at four and six respectively, and he tended the flower beds, kept the tennis courts in order, and saw that the trim paths were properly rolled and swept. He was an elderly man with a wife and a large family, and the small wage he received for his labours made just sufficient difference to his pension — he was an ex-sergeant of infantry — to keep a roof over his head and feed the hungry mouths that were dependent on him. Mr. Flock was a small man, with a thin, reddish-brown face, and a voice that was permanently husky from the gas which had played havoc with his vocal chords in 1917. He was a cheerful man in spite of his responsibilities, and the Square was his hobby as well as his job.

He was a little late on the Monday morning. He had spent Sunday night at the 'Load of Hay,' celebrating his birthday, and some hilarious wag had suggested that he should drink a glass of beer for every year of his age. He had got as far as eighteen when the proceedings no longer interested him. Reaching the Square he inserted his key in the lock of the west gate with a hand that was slightly shaky. His job that morning was the weeding of the large circular bed that occupied the centre of the smooth lawn. Closing the gate behind him, he made his way to his little lock-up shed where he kept his tools. His head was a little bit muzzy, but he hoped that the air would have the effect of clearing it. As he crossed the green strip of grass towards the bed, he reflected rather sorrowfully on the remarks that his wife had passed on the previous night, and repeated with additions that morning. And then he glanced at the oak tree on his left. The ruddiness left his face and he dropped his tools, staring with horrified eyes at the thing that swung gently from one of the lower branches. He felt his heart come leaping into his throat, and then he sighed with sudden relief. Of course, there was nothing there really. This was the result of those eighteen beers. If he closed his eyes the vision would go away. He closed his eyes very tightly, and then cautiously opened them again. The thing was still there. Mr. Flock nearly collapsed. His knees wobbled unpleasantly, and his throat felt suddenly dry and rough. He looked quickly from side to side, and then over his shoulder. He must tell the police at once ... And then a doubt assailed him. Supposing there really was nothing there after all? He'd look a nice fool ... He forced himself to go closer, and with every step he took it became more and more evident that this was no vision of a beer-disordered mind, but real. He was almost underneath the swaying horror now; could see the bloated face ... His nerve gave way, and with a hoarse yell he turned, and fled madly to the gate, reached it, opened it and dashed out of the Square as if all the fiends of hell were at his heels. And he never stopped until he reached the police station, and poured out his disjointed story to the incredulous ears of Sergeant Bolton.

'Bolton turned him over to Lightfoot,' said Shadgold, as he accompanied Trevor Lowe towards the police station, 'and then came along and informed me.'

'None of you has seen the body yet then?' said the dramatist.

Shadgold shook his head.

'I haven't,' he answered. 'I came straight along to fetch you. Lightfoot will be up there, of course.'

They found that this supposition was correct, for only Sergeant Bolton was waiting for them when they reached the police station.

'The inspector's gone up to the Square, sir,' he said. 'He asked me to bring you along.'

Shadgold nodded and heaved a sigh of relief as he saw the police car that was waiting to take them. He had had quite enough exercise for one day.

Ten minutes later they were standing beside Inspector Lightfoot gazing at the object that still hung suspended from the low branch of the tree.

'Have you identified him?' asked Lowe.

'Yes, sir,' answered Lightfoot. 'It's a man called George Tidd. Everybody round these parts called him 'Monkey' George.'

'Who was he?' grunted Shadgold.

'Rather a bad character from all accounts,' said the inspector. 'We was always having trouble with him.'

'Well, you won't have any more,' remarked the dramatist, eyeing the thing on the tree.

'We may as well cut him down, don't you think?' said Shadgold, and Lightfoot nodded.

'Yes,' he said, 'I was only waiting for you to see him.'

He gave an order to a constable, and in a few seconds the remains of 'Monkey' George, a pathetic spectacle, were laid out decently on the fresh grass.

'May I have a look at that rope?' asked Lowe, and it was passed to him.

He ran it through his fingers, frowned, and turned to Shadgold.

'There's nothing of any use here,' he remarked. 'It's ordinary clothes line. You could buy it at any shop that sells that sort of thing, and it's new. By the way, were the other ropes new?'

Lightfoot, who was bending over the body, heard him and looked round.

'Yes, sir,' he answered.

'Bought specially for the purpose,' murmured the dramatist.

He joined the local inspector by the body, and watched him while he searched the pockets.

'Anything useful?' asked Shadgold.

'Nothing so far,' replied Lightfoot. 'Only one or two snares. Hullo, here's something.'

He pulled out of the breast pocket of the ragged overcoat a square, white object, glanced at it, grunted and handed it to the Scotland Yard man. Shadgold's mouth set grimly as he looked at the pencilled words : 'With the compliments of The Hangman.' He passed the card on to Lowe.

'The murderer's signature tune!' he grunted.

'Apparently he's very anxious that nobody else shall get the credit for his crimes.'

'Yes, isn't he?' said the dramatist. 'Rather peculiar, don't you think?'

Shadgold shrugged his shoulders.

'Oh, I don't know,' he answered. 'It's vanity, I suppose. They're all as vain as turkey cocks.'

He looked round quickly as somebody rattled the gate.

'Hullo! Here's your police surgeon. Doctor Murford.'

The constable went over and unlocked the gate. The little doctor came hurriedly in, practically ignored Lowe and Shadgold, and addressed himself to Lightfoot.

'Got your call,' he said. 'What's all this? Another?'

'Looks like it,' said Lightfoot shortly.

Murford grunted, and dropped on to one knee beside the body.

'Good God!' he ejaculated as he saw

the face. 'It's that fellow Tidd! Why on earth should anyone want to kill him?' He looked fiercely from one to the other as though he really expected a reply.

'We don't know that, Doctor, any more than we know who killed him,' said Shadgold.

Murford grunted, shot him an unpleasant glance, and turned once more to the body. His examination was brief, and rising to his feet he brushed the knees of his trousers.

'Death was due to strangulation, same as the others,' he said curtly. 'You don't need me to tell you that.'

'Can you tell us how long he's been dead?' asked Lightfoot.

'Not less than four hours,' said the doctor. 'That's as near as I can put it.'

'That makes the time that he was killed somewhere before three o'clock,' remarked Shadgold, glancing at his watch.

The police surgeon nodded shortly.

'About that time,' he agreed. 'I can't be more accurate.'

'What time did the rain stop?' inquired the dramatist.

Apparently nobody knew, for they all shook their heads.

'If you can find that out,' said Lowe, 'it might help to fix the time more definitely. His clothes are soaked through.'

'That doesn't say he was dead when they got soaked through,' argued Doctor Murford. 'He could have got wet just as easily alive.'

'Quite,' murmured the dramatist. 'What I'm trying to point out, though, is that if for the sake of argument, the rain stopped at three let us say, then Tidd was killed before that time.'

Shadgold frowned.

'I don't quite follow you, Mr. Lowe,' he said.

Lowe went over to the dead man.

'Look here,' he said. 'The man's clothing is wet, but it's not wet evenly. It's considerably wetter in front than it is at the back. It's wetter because for some time he was lying on his back in the pouring rain.'

'I see,' Shadgold nodded. 'But that's — hullo, what have you found?'

To demonstrate his argument the

dramatist had turned the body gently over, and the stout inspector heard the smothered exclamation he gave.

'Only that he was not killed in this Square,' remarked Lowe. 'Look at this — and this.' He pointed to stains on the back of the ragged coat. 'That's tar,' he went on. 'Fresh tar, and there are several pieces of flint sticking to it. This man was killed, or was lying just after his death, on some place which had been freshly tarred, and sprinkled with broken flint.'

The constable, who had been staring with rapt attention, gave vent to an ejaculation.

'They've been tarrin' the cross roads!' he exclaimed. 'Tarred 'em Saturday, they did.'

Lightfoot looked at him sharply.

'You mean the cross roads up by Linden?' he asked.

The policeman nodded.

'Yes, sir,' he said. 'I was up that way while they was doin' 'em.'

'Then it was there or near there that the actual murder took place,' said Lowe. 'Unless they've been repairing the roads anywhere else in the district.'

'I'll soon find that out,' said Lightfoot. 'I'll put an inquiry through when we get back to the station.'

'If we can be certain that this man met his death at the cross roads,' said Shadgold, 'we might find something there that would help us.'

'Might I suggest,' said Lowe, 'that there's another clue that it would be as well to follow up without delay.' They looked at him inquiringly.

'What's that, sir?' asked Lightfoot.

'This garden is private property,' explained the dramatist. 'Whoever brought the body here and hanged it to that tree must have had a key.'

Lightfoot looked a little dubious.

'That applies to everyone living in the Square,' he said, shaking his head. 'All the residents have got keys — some of them more than one.'

'Then we must make house to house inquiries,' said Shadgold. 'This may be the means of narrowing our search for the killer down to one locality.'

Trevor Lowe pursed his lips.

'Keys are easily lost,' he said, 'but if you can find somebody living in this Square who has also lost part of one of his finger-nails, then I think the search will be over.'

13

The Third Finger

A stretcher was sent for from the police station and the body of 'Monkey' George was taken away to rest side by side with those other victims of the unknown killer. The trembling Mr. Flock, whose indiscretions of the previous night, combined with the shock of his discovery, had reduced almost to a state of hysteria, was sent home, after a close questioning had added nothing to his original story. Lowe and the others were debating among themselves where they should start on their house-to-house inquiries in the Square when a hail from the gate attracted their attention. Turning, they saw Major Payton. The chief constable was admitted and came over to the group excitedly.

'I got your message from the station, Lightfoot.' He greeted and nodded to

Lowe. 'This is a terrible business. Have you discovered anything?'

Lightfoot told him briefly and Payton frowned.

'So you think he was killed at these cross roads, eh?' he commented.

'That's Mr. Lowe's opinion, sir,' replied the inspector, 'and the fact that he was found in this garden certainly seems to point to somebody in the Square.'

'But that's impossible,' protested the chief constable. 'I know nearly everyone in the Square personally. They're most respectable people.'

Trevor Lowe smiled.

'So was Crippen,' he remarked. 'Some of the most callous murderers have been recruited from the ranks of respectable people. Respectability is after all only a very thin veneer.'

Payton made a grimace.

'I suppose there is something in that,' he agreed. 'But to think, to imagine that any of these people — ' He waved his hand in the direction of the surrounding houses. 'It's incredible, unbelievable!'

'It is equally unbelievable that these

people should have been hanged for apparently no reason,' said the dramatist. 'By the way, how long has Doctor Murford been at Hill Green?'

The chief constable shot him a surprised glance.

'Ever since the place was built,' he replied, 'and that's, let me see, getting on for three years. Why?'

'I'm rather interested in Doctor Murford,' said Lowe. He turned to Shadgold. 'Did you notice that he kept his glove on his injured hand this morning?'

The Scotland Yard man nodded, and Payton looked rather bewildered.

'Injured hand,' he said. 'What are you talking about?'

'Doctor Murford has some sort of injury to the second finger of his left hand,' said Lowe. 'We noticed it yesterday, he was wearing a finger-stall so it was impossible to see what was the matter.'

'Good God!' The chief constable was genuinely startled. 'Are you suggesting — '

'No,' broke in Lowe quickly. 'I'm not, but I'm naturally interested in anyone who has hurt their finger since the discovery of that nail.'

'But, Murford!' ejaculated Payton. 'He's the divisional-surgeon.'

'One of the greatest criminals that ever lived,' said the dramatist, 'was also a surgeon. Anyhow I'm not making any accusation against Doctor Murford. All I say is, that it's an odd coincidence.'

'I agree with you there,' said Payton. He looked at Lightfoot. 'Are you ready to begin this house-to-house inquiry?' he asked.

The local man nodded.

'Quite,' he answered. 'Are you willing to help us with it, Mr. Lowe?'

'I should like to,' answered the dramatist, 'and since there are three of us, we may as well split the business up between us. We can get it done quicker that way.'

'You mean each take a house,' said Shadgold. 'Yes, that's a good idea.'

'I'll be getting along, I think,' said Payton. 'There'll probably be an avalanche of phone calls and what not as soon as this latest tragedy becomes public. I'll see you later, Lightfoot.'

'Very good, sir,' replied the inspector. 'You'll find Sergeant Bolton at the station. He went back with the body.'

The chief constable nodded.

'Let me know directly you get on to anything, won't you?' he said. 'I hope to heaven we shall have something tangible soon. There's going to be the devil of a commotion over this last business.'

He bade them a hurried good-bye, and as soon as he had driven off in his little car, the others left the Square, locking the gate behind them.

'Now,' said Shadgold. 'We'll start these inquiries. I'll take the first house, you take the second, Lightfoot, and you, Mr. Lowe, the third. We'll go right round the Square in that order. What we want everybody to do is to account for their keys, and also to find out if they saw anything.'

It was a weary and monotonous job, and by the time the dramatist had done his fourth house, he was beginning to wish that he had not offered to help. The people of the Square were indignant at the tragedy that had happened in their select retreat; they were curious and apt to be talkative, one enterprising lady tried to secure Lowe's autograph; they were horrified and talked about the incompetence of the police, in fact they were everything but helpful. Lowe was shown a multitude of garden keys until he could have drawn the shape of the wards from memory. But every key so far was accounted for, and nothing about the people he had interviewed could be called suspicious. He wondered as he approached his fifth front door whether Lightfoot and Shadgold had been more successful. Of course, the whole thing was more a forlorn hope than anything else, even if the murderer was to be found among the residents of this Square, it was unlikely that he would do anything to give himself away. Except, of course, the broken finger-nail. He could not hide that even if he realized there was any need. Lowe's thoughts returned to Doctor Murford. He knew of the significance of the broken nail, he had heard Lowe relate the discovery to Payton over the phone. It had been after that that the dramatist had noticed his injured finger, and Murford had hurried away very quickly. A peculiar coincidence that, if nothing more. He opened the little white gate of the house next on his list, and walked up the drive. It was a nice house with a neat door, and neat curtains. In fact that adjective neat very aptly described it. He raised his hand and pressed the bell, there was a long interval and then the door was opened by an elderly silver-haired man, whom Lowe judged to be the butler. He looked at the dramatist inquiringly.

'Good morning,' said Lowe pleasantly. 'Could I have a word with the owner of this house?'

'Mr. Nethcott, sir?' said the old man. 'I think he's rather busy at the moment, but I'll see. What name shall I say, sir?'

'Lowe, Trevor Lowe,' replied the dramatist. 'Here is my card. I am helping the police in connection with the murder — '

He stopped, the old man had uttered a startled exclamation and his face had suddenly gone white.

'Will — will you come in, sir,' he quavered uneasily.

He stood aside and Lowe stepped across the threshold, noting as he did so that the servant's hand was shaking.

'If you will — will wait here, sir,' the old man indicated a chair, 'I will inquire if Mr. Nethcott will see you.'

He gave Lowe a frightened glance and went towards a door at the rear of the hall. He tapped, and after pausing for a moment, went in, closing the door behind him. Trevor Lowe frowned. Here was something odd. At the mention of his name and business he had seen fear in the old man's face and eyes. Now why was he afraid? It was not just the natural fear occasioned by the close proximity of a murder. It had been more than that. This man had something to hide. The dramatist felt a little excited. Had he at last stumbled on something? Before he could even answer the question in his mind, the door through which the old man had made his exit opened again, and as he came out Lowe heard somebody say, a woman: 'We'll have to be careful,' and then the butler was speaking:

'If you will come this way, sir,' he said,

'Mr. Nethcott will see you.'

The dramatist followed him as he led the way to the door, but he was thinking of what he had just overheard. Of what had these people to be careful? That phrase spoken in a low tone combined with the obvious agitation of the servant required an explanation, and seemed capable of only one. In some way the murder of poor 'Monkey' George affected these people.

The butler held open the door and entered the room beyond. It was a pleasant room, large and with just sufficient furniture to make it comfortable without overcrowding it. In front of the fireplace stood a short stoutish man, whose restlessness betrayed his unease. Over by the window that faced the garden was a girl, who turned quickly as the dramatist came in, obviously the owner of the voice that had said so swiftly and warningly: 'We shall have to be careful.' The little man before the fire-place bowed in greeting.

'Good morning,' he said, speaking a trifle jerkily. 'Lane tells me you wish to see me about this horrible business in the Square.' His face twitched, he was obviously keyed up to an unnatural pitch, his nerves on edge. That was plain.

'Yes,' answered the dramatist easily. 'I'm very sorry to trouble you, but I am helping the police to make inquiries at every house in the Square in the hope that some of the residents may have seen something.'

The sigh that came softly from the girl at the window sounded very much like a breath of relief.

'I'm afraid we can't help you,' Mr. Nethcott shook his head. 'We neither saw nor heard anything.'

'We went to bed early,' said the girl, 'so it was unlikely that we should.'

Lowe looked at her steadily.

'I don't think I mentioned anything about time,' he said, and she bit her lip in vexation.

'I meant,' she said quickly, 'that if — if this thing was done during the night — '

'Why should you think that it was done during the night?' broke in Lowe.

She reddened.

'I thought it was,' she answered sharply.

'I think I heard one of the servants say that it was.'

'When was the man killed?' asked Mr. Nethcott hastily.

'During the early hours of the morning?' answered the dramatist, and noted the quick look that passed between the two. 'So you neither of you saw anything, a car standing about for instance?'

'No, we saw nothing,' declared Nethcott.

'Nor any of your servants?' asked Lowe.

'You are at liberty to question them if you wish,' said the little man, 'but I don't think they could have seen anything, otherwise they would have mentioned it.'

'I should like to have a word with them presently,' said the dramatist. 'In the meanwhile would you tell me how many keys you have to the centre garden.'

'Keys?' Mr. Nethcott frowned.

Lowe nodded.

'We are trying to find out if any of the residents have lost a key lately,' he explained. 'The murderer must have had a key to get into the garden at all, and it will help if all the known keys can be accounted for.'

'Oh, I see, yes of course,' the little man nodded quickly. 'Let me think how many have we?'

'Three,' put in the girl quietly.

'Yes, that's right, Joyce,' Nethcott turned to her in relief. 'Three.'

'Could I see them?' asked Lowe.

'Certainly.' Mr. Nethcott pressed a bell at the side of the fire-place, and presently the butler answered the summons.

'Yes, sir,' he said respectfully.

'This — er — Mr. Lowe wants to see the keys of the centre garden, Lane,' said his master. 'Bring them, will you.'

'Yes, sir,' Lane bowed and withdrew, and there was a rather embarrassing silence.

The girl had gone back to the window and was looking idly out at the Square. Mr. Nethcott still occupied the centre of the hearthrug, but now he was playing nervously with his lips, pinching them between his forefinger and thumb.

Presently the butler came back.

'Here you are, sir,' he said, and at a gesture from the little man handed the keys to Lowe.

The dramatist looked at them.

'I thought you said there were three,' he remarked.

'That's right,' replied Nethcott.

'There are only two here,' said Lowe.

With a smothered exclamation the girl turned quickly from the window, and her face was white.

'Two?' she said incredulously. 'There are three, there must be three.'

Lowe held out his hand and pointed to the keys with their attached metal labels, bearing the name of the owner and the number of the house.

'Look for yourself,' he said.

'They were the only ones on the hook, Miss,' said Lane.

'But — ' began Joyce and stopped. 'I'll see if the other's in my bag.'

She left the room hurriedly, and while she was gone Lowe watched the varying expressions on the faces of Mr. Nethcott and the butler. The little man's jaw had dropped at the discovery that there were only two keys, but he had succeeded in partially recovering himself, and was now striving to look unconcerned. A lamentable effort which would not have

139

deceived a child. Lane was even less successful in hiding his emotions, his lined old face looked positively haggard, and his faded eyes kept on shooting little darting questioning glances from Lowe to his master and back again. Happening to catch the dramatist's eye during one of these, he flushed a deep red, and then went so white that for a moment Lowe thought he was going to faint. There was some secret shared by the inmates of this house. Their agitation — almost a guilty agitation — seemed to point definitely that these people had knowledge of — what? The identity of 'The Hangman'? Perhaps, or at least, if not actual knowledge a very great suspicion.

The door opened and Lowe, thinking it was the girl coming back, turned. As he did so he heard a little gasp from Lane, and saw that the butler's face was a grotesque mask of fear. And yet the man who had entered was mild enough. A thin man, younger than Nethcott, but sufficiently like him for Lowe to guess the relationship. A man who looked as if he had not slept properly for weeks, with a pallid face and dark circles under sunken eyes. He stood hesitating on the threshold, his restless gaze travelling from one to the other.

'I'm sorry,' he said, and his voice was very gentle, Lowe mentally described it as hushed. 'I had no idea there was anyone with you, Francis.'

Mr. Nethcott coughed.

'Er — come in Harold,' he said. 'Come in. This is my brother, Mr. Lowe.'

The newcomer bowed.

'Mr. Lowe has come,' the little man continued, 'to ask a few questions. There has — er — been a regrettable — er — occurrence in the Square, in the garden.'

'A murder was committed last night,' said Lowe gravely, 'and I am trying to find out if anybody in the Square saw anything.'

'Murder?' Harold Nethcott flinched and drew thin brows down over narrowed eyes. 'Another of these — hangings?' He hesitated over the last word and his brother broke in quickly:

'Yes, I didn't say anything to you about

it, because I know how it upsets you,' he said.

'It does upset me.' The other's hand went up to his mouth with a nervous gesture. 'I don't know why it should but it does. It horrifies me, and makes me feel quite ill. Why should it, I wonder?'

Trevor Lowe was not even listening, his eyes were fixed on that trembling hand, and particularly on the third finger.

Part of the nail had been torn away!

14

Colonel Hastings Makes Up His Mind

Colonel Hastings, the Governor of Widemoore Criminal Lunatic Asylum, read an account of the latest Hill Green tragedy in his evening newspaper. To be exact, he read it three times, and as a result was so abstracted and thoughtful during his dinner that his wife concluded that he must be on the verge of an illness. After the meal, he went to his office, where his secretary, Thompson, was working, and stopped that industrious man in the midst of a complicated report for the Home Office.

'There's been another murder at that Garden City place,' he said abruptly.

Thompson leaned back in his chair, removed his glasses and wiped them carefully on a silk handkerchief.

'So I saw in the papers, sir,' he answered.

The governor lit a cigarette and tossed the match into an ash-tray.

'Well, what are we going to do about it?' he demanded irritably.

'We?' The secretary raised his eyebrows inquiringly. 'I don't quite see, sir, what it has got to do with us.'

The colonel frowned, puffed savagely at his cigarette for a moment, and then hurled it into the fire-place.

'It's got everything to do with us,' he exclaimed. 'If you want to know, I think we're almost the only people in the world who are aware of the identity of the killer.'

Thompson replaced his glasses on the bridge of his thin nose with great deliberation.

'Meaning you think it's Smedley,' he said.

Hastings snorted.

'Think!' he snapped. 'I'm sure it's Smedley. I said when he left here a year ago that we should hear more about him, and I was right. This sudden outbreak of motiveless crimes proves it.'

The secretary shook his head slowly.

'That, sir,' he said, 'is rather a sweeping

statement, if you don't mind my saying so. You have no proof whatever that these murders were perpetrated by Smedley.'

'Only my own common sense!' growled the governor. 'And that's good enough for me. Don't you think it's Smedley?'

'I do and I don't, sir,' replied Thompson. 'What I mean is the method of the crimes certainly suggests Smedley; the fact that they are almost certainly the work of an insane man again suggests Smedley. But, and here I'm sure, sir, you will agree with me, they might just as easily have been committed by somebody else.'

'They might have been committed by the Rajah of Bungho, but they weren't!' retorted the colonel. 'No, Thompson, I am convinced that Smedley is the fellow. These murders are exact counterparts of the ones for which he was arrested twenty-one years ago. How many murderers have hanged their victims before, tell me that?'

'I can't recollect any at the moment, sir,' said Thompson.

'No,' growled Hastings, 'and you won't except Smedley. I'm as sure that he's the guilty man as if I'd seen him do it. And what's worrying me, is what I ought to do.'

'What can you do, sir?' asked the secretary.

'I can get in touch with the people at the Home Office or Scotland Yard and remind them that Smedley was let out a year ago,' answered the colonel. 'That's what I ought to do, and that's what I think I shall do.'

'Supposing,' said Thompson, 'that you did that, and that Smedley wasn't guilty after all. You'd practically be responsible for getting him back here, sir.'

'That's what's bothering me,' admitted the governor. 'That tiny little doubt. But, damn it all, man, we can't — I can't — stand by and do nothing while people are being killed every day.'

'Why not, sir?' asked Thompson coolly. 'It's not your job to interfere. The Yard people are aware that Smedley was released a year ago. Or if they haven't remembered it, it's up to them to do so. The Home Secretary knows, he signed the orders. If they haven't connected Smedley with these crimes, I don't see why you should help them.'

'Because it's the duty of every respectable citizen to help the police if he can,' grunted Hastings. 'I have certain information, which I feel it's my duty to divulge. After I've done that, then I agree with you that it's no longer any affair of mine.'

There was a long pause before the secretary replied, and when he did it was to ask a question.

'I suppose you haven't any idea where Smedley is, sir?' he asked. The colonel shook his head.

'Not the least,' he replied, 'but I'm willing to bet that he's somewhere near this place, Hill Green.'

Thompson smiled to himself. The 'old man' wasn't going to give up his theory. He was as obstinate as a mule.

Hastings helped himself to another cigarette, and began to pace up and down the office, smoking, and after a little while the secretary went back to his work. He had typed four foolscap sheets of the intricate report when his employer stopped him.

'Get the Yard,' he snapped suddenly, 'and see if I can speak to the Assistant Commissioner. I've made up my mind. I'm going to tell them what I think and then it'll be off my conscience.'

Thompson obediently drew the telephone towards him, asked for Trunks and gave Scotland Yard's number. There was a slight delay in getting through, and more delay in getting connected with the Assistant Commissioner, but presently he handed the receiver to Hastings.

'Here you are, sir,' he said, and sighed. He had done his best to prevent the governor from interfering, he could do no more.

'Hallo!' barked the colonel. 'This is the governor of Widemoore Asylum speaking. I have some information to give you relating to the Hill Green murders.' He began to speak rapidly, and the result of his telephone conversation was to cause several people not a little trouble and anxiety, including that well-known dramatist, Mr. Trevor Lowe.

15

The Hangman?

Trevor Lowe found great difficulty in removing his eyes from that jagged and broken nail on the hand of Harold Nethcott. Had he, by sheer accident, found the murderer, the man who called himself 'The Hangman'? Was this small, almost frail man responsible for the killing of three people? It was almost incredible, and yet the broken nail could scarcely be a coincidence. Not that Lowe was a disbeliever in coincidence, he had seen too many in the course of his life to be a scoffer, and he knew that they were more common than the average person admits. But this, combined with the air of secrecy which the people of this household possessed, and the missing key, was too incredible a coincidence to be thought of. The dramatist's lips set a little sternly, but otherwise he gave no outward sign that he had noticed anything unusual.

'I suppose,' Harold Nethcott went on apologetically, 'that I am ultra sensitive, but really ever since I heard about these crimes I've felt queer. A kind of sick apprehension. I can't explain it.'

'You never were very strong,' murmured Mr. Nethcott. 'Why don't you go and lie down for a little while, Harold? You don't look at all well.'

His brother made a gesture of impatience.

'I'm quite all right physically,' he replied. 'It's inside my head — this thing that bothers me. I keep trying to remember something and I can't.'

His face clouded and he passed his hand across his forehead.

'It's as if there were something loose wandering about my brain, and I can't say what it is. I only know that it's something unpleasant, and any mention of these murders aggravates it.'

Lowe watched his troubled eyes sympathetically. The man was strung up, nervous, on the verge of a breakdown, but there was nothing guilty about him. If Harold

Nethcott had committed the crimes that had sent Hill Green into a panic, Lowe was willing to stake his reputation that he was not aware of the fact. If he were 'The Hangman' then he was suffering from some form of amnesia, and the memory of the murders had been completely erased from his consciousness except for that peculiar feeling of disgust that he had described.

'You saw nothing last night?' he asked, and Harold Nethcott shook his head.

'No, I saw nothing,' he replied. 'I couldn't very well have seen anything. I wasn't here.'

A sound, a smothered ejaculation of mingled surprise and consternation came from the lips of his brother.

'You weren't here?' he echoed. 'What do you mean, Harold?'

The other smiled.

'I was out,' he replied simply. 'I couldn't sleep, I haven't been sleeping well lately, and so I went for a walk.'

'Good heavens!' exclaimed the little man. 'In all that rain?'

'I put on a macintosh,' said his brother, 'and really it was rather pleasant and refreshing.'

'What time did you go out?' asked Lowe quietly.

'That I couldn't tell you,' admitted the other. 'Some time after midnight, I think. I got back shortly before three o'clock.'

'You must have walked a long way,' remarked the dramatist.

'I did,' answered Harold Nethcott. 'I wanted to see if I could tire myself out.'

At that moment the door opened and Joyce came back.

'The key is not in my bag,' she said. 'I've looked everywhere for it but I can't find it.'

The dramatist's face was grave.

'Can anyone tell me when they were all last seen together?' he asked.

No one could tell him. There had been three keys and now there were only two, but where the third had gone no one could say.

Lowe eventually took his leave. At the corner of the Square he met Shadgold and Inspector Lightfoot.

'Well,' he greeted. 'Have you found anything?'

The Scotland Yard man grunted and shook his head.

'Nothing much,' he answered. 'Somebody thought they heard a car in the Square a little after four, but they weren't sure. What about you?'

Lowe looked at him, and there was a perceptible pause before he replied.

'I think I've found the murderer,' he said quietly.

16

The Key

Inspector Lightfoot's office at the little police station was a fairly large room, but its holding capacity that afternoon was strained to the utmost. Major Payton, hastily summoned from his lunch, occupied Lightfoot's chair at the shabby ink-stained desk, and Lowe, Lightfoot, himself and Shadgold were seated in chairs commandeered for that purpose from the charge-room. The whole party were looking grave. Lowe had just finished giving an account of his visit to Nethcott's house, and following his recital, there was a dead silence broken at last by the chief constable.

'It's incredible,' he said in a low voice. 'I know these people well. In fact only last week I had dinner with them. I can't believe that Harold Nethcott can be the murderer.'

'It may be difficult to believe, sir,' said

Shadgold, 'but the evidence seems to be fairly conclusive. In fact, sufficient to justify applying for a warrant.'

Inspector Lightfoot nodded slowly.

'I think that too, sir,' he remarked.

'But why in the world should he kill these people?' exploded Major Payton. 'Can you tell me that?'

'The man is without question unbalanced,' said Trevor Lowe. 'I don't think he's quite responsible for his actions. I'm sure that he's not aware that he's killed anyone. Mention of the murders worries him. But he can't say why, and I'm inclined to believe that he's perfectly genuine.'

'Do you mean to tell me,' said the chief constable, 'that a man could go round hanging people and not know that he's done it?'

'Certainly,' replied the dramatist. 'It is quite possible. Any doctor will tell you so. I have also found out that for the past week Harold Nethcott has been in the habit of taking long walks at night because he couldn't sleep. He was out on each occasion when a murder was committed.'

The chief constable rolled a pencil up and down Inspector Lightfoot's blotting-pad.

'There seems very little doubt, I must admit,' he muttered. 'But I wouldn't like to do anything in a hurry. There may be some mistake. After all, circumstantial evidence has proved to be wrong on more than one occasion and there is such a thing as a coincidence.

He broke off, looked at Shadgold, transferred his gaze from that wooden countenance to Lightfoot, received no encouragement there, and finally looked at Lowe.

'There is such a thing as one coincidence,' admitted the dramatist. 'But scarcely as many as in the present instance.'

'I don't think we need look any farther,' grunted Shadgold.

'All the same,' Lowe continued, 'I rather agree with Major Payton about acting precipitantly. I think with the information you already possess you ought to be able to prove your case up to the hilt before you make the final move and arrest the man.'

Payton heaved a sigh of relief.

'I'm glad to hear you say that, Mr. Lowe,' he said. 'I suppose I ought not to take the matter into consideration, but — well these people are friends of mine, and I should like to make definitely sure that there can be no mistake.'

Lowe nodded.

'I should feel the same way myself,' he said.

'In the meanwhile, the man will get away, or murder someone else,' growled the Scotland Yard man.

'Oh no, he won't,' said Inspector Lightfoot grimly. 'I've got a man watching the house, with instructions to follow Nethcott wherever he goes.'

Shadgold brightened visibly, and the chief constable nodded.

'I think that was a wise move,' he said.

'In my opinion,' said the stout inspector, 'the finger-nail is the best bit of evidence we've got. It practically clinches the matter, and would be quite sufficient to convince a jury.'

The chief constable rubbed his chin gloomily.

'It will be a terrible thing for his brother and the girl,' he began, and was interrupted by the entrance of Sergeant Bolton.

'About that tar, sir,' he said, addressing Lightfoot, 'the only place where there's been any tar used recently is up at Linden cross roads.'

'Then that's where you'll find Tidd was killed,' interjected Lowe. 'Don't you think it would be a good idea to have a look at the place.'

'Not much point in that now, is there, Mr. Lowe?' said Shadgold, and the dramatist shrugged his shoulders.

'That's for you to say,' he remarked. 'But you never know what you might find. Besides, I thought you had decided to try and find all evidence you possibly could.'

The Scotland Yard man looked rather dubious but rose to his feet.

'We may as well go along there now, then,' he said. 'The longer we leave it, the more likely it is that any traces there are will be effaced.'

'I'll drive you there,' volunteered

Payton. 'I've got my car outside.'

They came out of the little police station, and squeezed into the chief constable's car.

It was a fair distance to the cross roads, but Payton drove without considering speed limits, and landed them at their destination in under twenty minutes.

'Lonely sort of place,' remarked Lowe as he got down, and stared about him. 'Particularly at night, and such a night as last night.'

A triangular patch of grass occupied the centre where the four roads met, from the middle of which stuck up a sign-post. Ahead was a wide expanse of ploughed field that ended in a thick belt of trees. Straggling hedges lined the road along which they had come. There was no sign of life anywhere. As the dramatist remarked, it was a lonely place, and ideal for the purpose to which it had been put. The repairs were plainly visible, and stretched for some hundreds of yards along the main road, but only a comparatively short distance along the secondary road.

Shadgold surveyed the tarred surface

with a gloomy face and pursed lips.

'We shan't find much here,' he commented. 'In spite of the rain this stuff doesn't hold marks. At least not marks that are going to be of any use to us.'

He allowed his eyes to wander over the grey expanse.

'There are one or two tyre impressions,' he continued, 'but that's all.'

Lowe was looking about in silence, walking slowly along towards the grass island where the roads intersected. Major Payton remained in his car watching interestedly, and presently he saw the dramatist stop, and peer more closely at the ground at his feet.

'Found something, Mr. Lowe?' he called.

Trevor Lowe straightened up and looked round.

'Nothing much,' he replied. 'There are signs of a small car having stopped here for some time. The tyres have sunk into the tar.'

'Somebody stopping to read the sign-post, most likely,' suggested Shadgold, but Lowe shook his head.

'It seems to have stopped too long for

that,' he said. 'More likely, if it was nothing to do with the murder, it was a breakdown.' He looked across at the chief constable. 'Have the Nethcotts got a car?' he asked.

'Yes,' answered Payton, 'a Comet coupé.'

'I didn't see any garage at the house,' said the dramatist. 'Where do they keep it?'

'They used to keep it at the garage at Hill Green,' answered Payton, 'but about three months ago a shed became empty near the Square, and Nethcott thought it would be more convenient to rent that.'

Lowe looked interested.

'Then it would be possible for any one of them to take the car out without anybody being the wiser,' he said.

'Yes, quite,' said the chief constable.

The dramatist pulled thoughtfully at his nose.

'The car that stopped here had a small patch on the nearside back wheel,' he remarked, 'the tyres were Dunlops non-skid.' He turned to Shadgold. 'It would be interesting to see the car that belongs to the Nethcotts.'

161

'I'll attend to that, sir,' put in Lightfoot, 'this evening.'

'There doesn't seem to be anything else here,' remarked Shadgold, 'so we may as well be getting back. Hullo, what's that?'

He walked over to the side of the road and picked up from among a tuft of weeds a small packet. It was dirty and sodden with rain. He carried it over to the others.

'What is it?' asked Payton as he approached.

'A parcel wrapped in brown paper and tied with string,' answered the inspector frowning, and turning it over in his fingers. 'I wonder what it is and how it got here.'

'Sandwiches that somebody has thrown away,' suggested the chief constable, 'that's what it looks like.'

'Suppose you open it and see,' remarked Lowe, and taking a penknife from his pocket, he held it out to Shadgold.

The Scotland Yard man cut the string, and unwrapped the brown paper and then he laughed. Inside was a wad of neatly-folded newspapers.

'What a sell!' he said, and was going to throw the whole thing away when Lowe stopped him.

'It's rather suggestive, don't you think?' said the dramatist.

'Suggestive of what?' asked Shadgold.

'Well,' said Lowe, 'why should anyone have taken so much trouble to make a neat parcel of old newspapers.'

'For a practical joke, I should imagine,' smiled the chief constable.

'Or perhaps,' said the dramatist, 'to make somebody think that it contained something of value.'

'Well, anyway,' said Shadgold impatiently, 'it can't have anything to do with our business.'

'Maybe it hasn't,' murmured Lowe, 'on the other hand it might. I think I should keep it, Shadgold, if I were you.'

The stout inspector looked at him, hesitated, and then with a shrug thrust the sodden mass into his overcoat pocket.

'Well, what about getting back?' he said. 'We're only wasting time here.'

They drove back to the police station,

and as they entered the charge-room Sergeant Bolton greeted them with an air of suppressed excitement.

'We've made a discovery, while you've been away, sir,' he said, addressing Lightfoot. 'One of our men 'as found the key.'

'Key? What key?' snapped the inspector.

'The key the murderer used to open the garden gate,' answered his subordinate.

'Where was it found?' put in Shadgold quickly.

'In a corner of the Square, sir,' answered Bolton, 'lying in the gutter.'

He went over to a desk, opened a drawer and took out a small object.

''Ere it is,' he said, 'an' what's more it's got the name of the owner on this little metal label!'

He held it out and they grouped round him.

'I think that removes the last doubt, if there ever was a doubt,' remarked Shadgold.

The name on the label was Nethcott.

17

The Arrest

Owing to the small staff at Hill Green police station, the two men whom Shadgold had brought down with him from London were put temporarily at the service of the local police. Larson was therefore given the job of examining the Nethcotts' car, and reporting on the state of the tyres. And Nares towards evening was sent to relieve the man who was watching the Nethcott house.

Whatever slight doubt Trevor Lowe might have had regarding Harold Nethcott's guilt had been completely dispelled by the discovery of the key. Every fresh clue, small though they were, pointed to the fact that he was the murderer. After returning from the cross roads and learning of the finding of the key, Shadgold, the chief constable and Inspector Lightfoot had had a short conference to which the dramatist had been invited; and the result of that conference was to send Lightfoot in search of a certain Mr. Crablett, who was also the chief magistrate for the district, to swear out a warrant for the arrest of Harold Nethcott.

'We'll take him to-night,' mumbled Shadgold, his mouth full of beef sandwich which had been sent in to the station.

Lowe nodded, but his face was a little troubled.

'What's the matter, Mr. Lowe?' demanded the Scotland Yard man, 'you look pretty glum.'

The dramatist helped himself to a sandwich from the heaped pile, and shrugged his shoulders. They were alone, for Payton had taken his departure with Lightfoot.

'I don't like it at all, Shadgold,' he admitted after a pause.

The stout inspector stared at him in surprise.

'Don't like what?' he said with difficulty.

'The whole business,' answered Lowe, shaking his head. 'It's nasty. I wish I wasn't mixed up with it.'

'Do you mean that you don't think that this man Nethcott is guilty?' asked Shadgold.

'No, no,' replied the dramatist quickly. 'I don't think there's any doubt of that. But I'm equally convinced that he's not responsible for his actions.'

'That's nothing to do with us,' growled the inspector. 'That's for the doctors, and the judge and the jury to decide. Our job was to find the man responsible for these murders, and we've done it.'

Lowe smiled wryly.

'There wasn't much to do, was there?' he said. 'It was all done for us. Anyway, I'm glad it's over, it's been a most unsavoury business and the worst part's to come.'

In his mind's eye he saw the little harassed, nervous man who was the brother of the man they were going to arrest. It would be a terrible shock to him, and to that girl. They had suspected, of course, that was why they had been so scared. But that wouldn't mitigate the force of the blow.

'I suppose you'll be going back to town

to-night, Mr. Lowe,' said Shadgold presently.

'Yes, I think so,' replied the dramatist. 'I'll give you a lift if you like.'

'I shan't go back till to-morrow, thanks all the same,' said the Scotland Yard man. 'I'd like to thank you, Mr. Lowe, for coming down and giving me a hand. Bringing this affair to a successful climax is going to do me a bit of good at headquarters.'

'As things turned out you would have done just as well on your own,' answered the dramatist. 'Finish the sandwiches: I don't want any more.'

Shadgold obeyed with alacrity. He was just eating the last crumb when Lightfoot came in.

'I've got it,' he announced. 'When shall we go and pull the fellow in?'

'Might as well go now, and get it over,' said Shadgold, rising to his feet. 'Are you coming, Mr. Lowe?'

Lowe shook his head, and then for some reason which he was never able to account for, he changed his mind.

'Yes I will,' he said quickly, and

followed Shadgold and the inspector out to the police car.

The Square was dark and gloomy when they came to a halt before the Nethcotts' house. As they got out a man detached himself from the shadows and came towards them.

'Anything to report, Nares?' asked Shadgold.

'No, sir,' said the watcher, 'nothing special. Our man's inside, and about half an hour ago a young fellow called.'

The Scotland Yard man nodded shortly.

'All right.' He turned to Lightfoot. 'Are you ready, Inspector?'

The local man inclined his head, and Shadgold thrust open the gate. Followed by Lowe and Lightfoot, he made his way up to the front door. He had scarcely removed his hand from the bell when the door was opened, and silhouetted against a flood of yellow light Lane peered out at them. He recognized Lowe and his face changed. He made a quick movement as though to shut the door, thought better of it, and waited inquiringly.

'I am Detective-Inspector Shadgold of

Scotland Yard,' said that individual, 'and I want to see Mr. Harold Nethcott. Is he in?'

The butler's face was grey as he stood aside.

'If you will come in, sir,' he muttered with a slight shake in his voice, 'I'll see.'

They crossed the threshold and grouped themselves in the hall. Lane closed the door, hesitated for a second, and then walked slowly across the hall towards the door of the room in which Lowe had had his interview in the morning.

'That fellow looked as if he had expected us,' whispered Shadgold to Lowe. 'Did you see his face?'

The dramatist made no reply. He was certain that Lane had expected them.

He watched the old man as he raised his hand, tapped at the door, and after waiting a second went in. As the door opened there came the low hum of voices, which ceased suddenly. There was a startled exclamation, a smothered cry, and then Mr. Francis Nethcott came out. He came hurriedly, excitedly, his face drawn, and his fingers twitching.

'What's all this? What's all this?' he demanded angrily. 'You wish to see my brother. I'm sorry but you can't! We gave all the information we could to — er — this gentleman this morning.' He jerked his head towards Lowe. 'We cannot be continually pestered in this way. It's outrageous!'

'I'm afraid, sir,' said Shadgold gently when this outburst had subsided, 'that we have not come on this occasion for information.'

Lowe heard a sudden gasp from the door through which Francis Nethcott had entered. Standing in the doorway, her face white, was the girl Joyce. Behind her hovered a young man.

'You have — not come — for information?' stammered Mr. Nethcott. 'Then may I ask what you have come for?'

'I'm afraid I'm going to give you an unpleasant shock, sir,' said Shadgold apologetically. 'I have come to execute a warrant for your brother's arrest on a charge of murder.'

The sallow, strained face of the little

man went a dirty yellow. He staggered as though someone had given him a heavy blow, and something very like a groan escaped his ashen lips. The girl came hurriedly forward and put an arm round his neck.

'Pops,' she said huskily.

He recovered himself, and putting up a hand patted her arm.

'I'm all right, Joyce,' he muttered, and then: 'They've come — for Harold.'

Her face was pale, but she kept her composure.

'Come for Uncle Harold?' she said. 'What do you mean?'

'The police,' said Nethcott jerkily. 'They think — they think he's responsible for these murders.' He stopped, and the girl looked up, letting her glance stray from one to the other.

'But how absurd!' she exclaimed angrily. 'Uncle Harold of all people! It's ridiculous!'

Lowe felt a sudden admiration for her courage. She was bluffing gamely, but she knew. He could see she knew. This was no unexpected shock; it was something she had dreaded for a long time. Dreaded yet expected.

'I'm sorry, Miss,' began Shadgold, 'but — '

'Of course there's some mistake,' she interrupted. 'It's perfectly absurd that you should suspect my uncle.'

The Scotland Yard man looked uncomfortable. These were the sort of scenes he hated, and in spite of his experience he had never got used to them.

'There may be a mistake, Miss,' he replied, 'but that's for other people to decide. On the evidence we've got, it's my duty to arrest Mr. Nethcott. If you will allow me to see him — '

She turned on Lowe, her eyes suddenly hard and accusing.

'I suppose this is your doing,' she said contemptuously, and her voice was like ice. Ice with a core of tempered steel. 'That's why you came here this morning. I have heard of you. Why don't you attend to your own business? You're nothing to do with the police. You have a great reputation as a playwright. Isn't that enough for you? Why do you mix yourself up with this kind of thing? I demand to know what this concocted evidence is that you and the police have hatched up between you.'

'There is no concocted evidence,' answered Lowe, the colour in his face a little deeper, 'the evidence against your uncle, sorry as I am to say so, is conclusive. I certainly should not connect myself with what is commonly called a frame-up, neither would my friend, Inspector Shadgold.'

'What is it, Joyce?' A fresh voice interrupted the proceedings as the young man who had been lurking in the background came forward. 'Are these fools accusing Mr. Nethcott of being 'The Hangman'?'

She nodded.

'But,' he turned to Shadgold, 'surely there must be some mistake.'

'I'm afraid there isn't, sir,' answered the stout inspector patiently. 'We hold several clues and they all point to Mr. Harold Nethcott.'

'Is anything the matter?' a gentle voice broke in on his sentence and they looked up.

Harold Nethcott, pale, with dark circles

under his eyes, looking even frailer in his dinner-suit than he had done when Lowe had seen him that morning, was half way down the staircase. Joyce choked back a little sob.

'Come down, Harold,' said Mr. Nethcott huskily, 'these — er — people wish to speak to you.'

'To me?' The pale man raised his eyebrows as he came down the rest of the stairs. 'Why do they wish to speak to me?'

Shadgold cleared his throat and took a step forward.

'Your name is Harold Nethcott,' he said and the other nodded. 'I have a warrant here for your arrest on the charge of wilful murder,' went on the Scotland Yard man, 'and I must warn you that anything you say may be taken down and later used in evidence — '

Trevor Lowe sprang forward. He was just in time to catch the girl as she fainted.

18

For the Defence

With the assistance of the young man, Lowe carried her into the drawing-room and laid her on the settee by the fireplace. The old butler brought brandy, and in a few minutes she had recovered.

'Have — have they gone?' she asked, sitting up and smoothing her hair.

Lowe shook his head.

'No, not yet,' he answered. 'They're in the dining-room with Mr. Nethcott.' He turned to the young man. 'If you will look after Miss Elliot,' he said, 'I'll join them.'

Jim Bryant nodded.

'Mr. Lowe,' the girl's voice stayed him as he was crossing to the door. 'Will they — will they be taking Uncle Harold away to-night?'

'I'm afraid they will,' answered Lowe gently.

'Oh!' She dropped her eyes and stared at the floor.

The dramatist hesitated a moment, and then seeing that she had nothing more to say to him, he quietly went out and made his way to the dining-room. Lightfoot and Shadgold were standing just inside the door, Francis Nethcott occupied his favourite position in front of the fireplace. His brother was sitting a worried and dejected figure in an easy chair facing all three of them. They looked at Lowe as he entered.

'How is Joyce?' asked Mr. Nethcott anxiously.

'She is better,' replied the dramatist.

The man in the chair uttered a little sigh.

'Poor child,' he murmured, 'this must have given her a terrible shock.' He looked at Lowe with a faint smile. 'Do you believe that I am responsible for these atrocious crimes?' he asked suddenly.

The dramatist hesitated, and then before he could reply, Harold Nethcott went on:

'I see that you do,' he said quietly. 'Well, if I am, I assure you I have no knowledge of my guilt.'

'Don't worry, Harold,' put in his brother. 'You can rest assured that no effort will be spared to prove your innocence.'

'I'm not worrying about that,' was the reply.

'I'm sure you quite realize, sir,' said Shadgold, 'that in the circumstances we could act in no other way.'

'Yes, I realize that, now that I've heard the evidence against my brother,' said Mr. Nethcott reluctantly. 'I suppose you will want him to — to go with you to the police station.'

'Yes, sir,' replied Shadgold. 'We have a car outside and as soon as Mr. Nethcott is ready — '

He was interrupted by a tap on the door and the entrance of Lane.

'Excuse me, sir,' said the butler, addressing his master, 'but there is someone on the telephone for Detective-Inspector Shadgold.'

'For me?' said the Scotland Yard man in surprise.

'Yes, sir,' answered Lane. 'From the police station, sir.'

'I wonder what it's about,' muttered Shadgold. 'Where is your phone?'

'In the hall, sir.' The butler held open the door. 'If you will follow me, sir, I'll show you.'

Shadgold went out, and presently they heard the sound of his voice at the telephone. Nobody spoke while he was away. Lightfoot with official stolidity gaped at nothing. The man in the chair, his brows drawn together over his sunken eyes, had dropped into a reverie. His brother before the fire-place shifted uneasily from one foot to another, and pulled jerkily at a loose piece of flesh under his chin. Shadgold's conversation was a long one, and when he came back his face had changed. It was sterner and graver. He closed the door behind him, and stood for a moment looking from one to the other, then he spoke.

'Scotland Yard has been trying to get me at the station,' he said. 'A certain item of information has come into their possession that they thought necessary to pass on to me at once.' He stopped and rubbed at his small moustache. 'I should like a few words with you, Mr. Nethcott, in private, if you don't mind, if there is anywhere we can go.'

Francis Nethcott's face was even paler than before as he said quickly:

'Come into my study, Inspector.'

'Will you come too, Mr. Lowe?' said Shadgold. 'Inspector Lightfoot can stay here.'

Lowe nodded wonderingly, and followed Francis Nethcott and Shadgold into the hall.

'This way,' said the little man, and began to mount the staircase.

Opening a door on the first landing, he switched on the lights, and ushered them into a large plainly-furnished room.

'Now,' he said when he had closed the door, 'what is it, Inspector?'

Shadgold came straight to the point.

'Mr. Nethcott,' he said, 'was your brother once known as Harold Smedley?'

Lowe checked an exclamation, and Francis Nethcott appeared to shrink until he seemed even more haggard than before. His answer when it came was so low as to be barely audible.

'Yes,' he muttered.

'Until a year ago he was confined in Widemoore Asylum,' the Scotland Yard man went on. 'He was confined there because twenty years previously he killed his wife and child. At the trial, on the evidence of two specialists he was found to be insane, and so escaped the death sentence. The method he used to kill his wife and child was the same as in the present case. He hanged them.'

Francis Nethcott licked his dry lips.

'Yes,' he whispered huskily, 'but a year ago he was released. They said he had recovered, and on condition that I promised to look after him they let him out.'

'I know,' Shadgold nodded. 'The governor of Widemoore telephoned Scotland Yard after reading about the latest murder here, and they at once got into touch with me.' His voice took on a sterner note. 'Knowing this, Mr. Nethcott, it was your duty to have told the police about your brother.'

Francis Nethcott looked up and his eyes flashed.

'My duty to whom?' he demanded harshly.

'To the community at large,' retorted Shadgold. 'If we had known this before we might have saved the lives of Tidd and Miss Mortimer.'

'I was not certain that my brother had anything to do with the murders,' said the little man. 'I'm not certain now. I can't bring myself to believe anything so terrible. And if he was innocent, and I had revealed his past it would have been sufficient to stamp him as guilty.'

'There's no doubt about his guilt,' said Shadgold. 'It's obvious that in spite of the medical report he never really recovered.'

'I'm afraid there can be no doubt, Mr. Nethcott,' interjected Lowe quietly as he saw the distress on the other's face. 'It's a very dreadful business and very sad, because I'm certain that your brother has no knowledge that he has killed these people.'

'The verdict will almost certainly be 'guilty but insane,'' said Shadgold. 'Of course, he will have to be examined by a specialist appointed by the defence in consultation with one from the Home Office. That is the only consolation I can offer you, Mr. Nethcott.'

'And he will be sent back to — to Widemoore?' muttered Francis Nethcott brokenly.

'That I'm afraid is inevitable,' agreed Lowe.

The little man stood with bowed head for a moment, and then suddenly he squared his shoulders and looked up.

'Mr. Lowe,' he said earnestly, 'I have heard a lot about you. In one or two cases you have helped the police and been successful. Although everything seems to be against my brother, I personally am by no means convinced that he is guilty, and I shall do all in my power to prove that he is not.' He paused for a second as though considering his next words. 'You came down, I believe, to help your friend Inspector Shadgold with this dreadful affair. Would it be too much to ask you to remain and look into the matter for me?'

The dramatist was silent. He was rather at a loss to answer this request. In his heart he had no doubt at all regarding Harold Nethcott's guilt.

'I'm afraid I must decline,' he replied

slowly. 'Candidly I do not share your belief in your brother's innocence. If I did I would do all I could to help you, but the evidence is too strong to admit of doubt.'

Francis Nethcott's eyes clouded.

'I beg your pardon for asking you, Mr. Lowe,' he said a little stiffly. 'I shall, however, engage the best counsel I can obtain for the defence, and I would have liked you to have worked with him. If Harold is guilty, then much as it will grieve me, I can wish nothing else than he should be placed under restraint. If on the other hand he is not, I feel that nothing should be left undone to save him from the disgrace and suffering that will inevitably ensue. That was all I was asking you to do, since you have before been successful in similar cases.'

There was another silence. Shadgold shifted impatiently on his feet, while Lowe stared at the fingers of his left hand with knitted brows. Presently he raised his eyes and looked steadily at Mr. Nethcott.

'I am prepared to do one thing if it will satisfy you,' he said.

A small gleam of hope showed for a

moment in the little man's tired eyes.

'What is that?' he asked quickly.

'I will continue to look into this affair,' said the dramatist, 'on the condition that whatever I find I make public. I will not act solely for the defence, and suppress any further evidence that might strengthen the case against your brother. Whatever I discover, if anything, must be placed at the disposal of the proper authorities.'

Francis Nethcott hesitated for the fraction of a second, and then he nodded.

'Very well,' he said. 'I agree — and thank you.'

'And now, sir,' said Shadgold, breaking in impatiently. 'We had better go back to Mr. — er — er — Smedley, and get him to prepare to accompany me to the police station.'

19

White Has an Idea

The arrest of Harold Smedley, alias Nethcott, provided Hill Green with an even greater sensation than the murders. The carriages of the 8.20 were little cells of animated discussion. Mr. Stott from the corner of his first-class compartment expressed his views to a group of interested listeners, and talked as one having an inside knowledge of the affair.

'I'm not at all surprised,' he said, shaking his head profoundly. 'Not at all surprised. Those people up at the Square are a peculiar lot. That girl, for instance, always flying about here, there and everywhere with that fellow Bryant, and they're not even engaged. It's not right, you know. I wouldn't allow a daughter of mine to behave like that.'

His listeners, whose daughters mostly did as exactly as they liked, agreed with him that it was not right.

'And then these Smedleys living there all this time under an assumed name,' Mr. Stott continued, 'that's a bit of an eye-opener for some of them. Fancy having a crazy man, who had already murdered two people, wandering loose about the place. It's disgraceful! I rather think the authorities will get into trouble over that.'

He continued in the same strain until the train drew into Waterloo, and discharged its cargo, scattering them to the four winds of heaven.

Trevor Lowe, breakfasting at the 'Hillside Hotel,' heard the matter discussed by various members of the staff and frowned. He had ordered his car for nine o'clock with the intention of going back to London. That he had not gone on the previous night had been due to Francis Nethcott, who had insisted on his remaining behind after Shadgold and Lightfoot had taken Harold Smedley away, to discuss in more detail the task that Lowe had undertaken. The result had not been helpful in any way, but Lowe had arrived back at the hotel much too

187

late and too tired to think of going back to London that night. In his own mind he was certain that no amount of investigation would help Harold Smedley in the least, and the more he thought about it the more he became annoyed with himself for having agreed to do what he had. It was, he felt, going to be a complete waste of time, and at the moment he had no idea where to make a start. The evidence against Smedley was absolutely conclusive. His past, the broken nail, the key, the fact that he was out on each occasion when a crime had been committed, and finally — a fact he had learned that morning over the telephone from Shadgold — that the car owned by the Nethcotts had a patched tyre coinciding with the impressions that had been found at Linden cross roads. In face of all this evidence it seemed futile to attempt to find anything for the defence. Lowe candidly admitted that he had not the remotest idea how to make a start.

He finished his breakfast, paid his bill, and went out to his waiting car. The porter brought his suit-case, accepted a tip with a smiling salute, and the dramatist drove away. Acting on an impulse he called at the police station. Shadgold and Lightfoot were in the charge-room, and the Scotland Yard man looked surprised to see him.

'Hallo, Mr. Lowe!' he greeted. 'I thought you were on your way to London.'

'So I am,' said Lowe smiling, 'but I've just thought of something. Have you got the reports about the past lives of Doctor Wallington and Miss Mortimer?'

It was Lightfoot who answered.

'Yes, sir,' he said, 'the last one came in this morning.'

'I wonder,' asked Lowe, 'if you could let me have copies of them?'

Lightfoot looked at Shadgold and the Scotland Yard man wrinkled his nose.

'You can have copies of them, if you want them,' he said. 'What's the idea, Mr. Lowe?'

'Nothing particular,' replied the dramatist, 'only I'd just like to glance through them. When can I have the copies?'

'Well, I shall have to get them made, sir,' said Lightfoot. 'We've only one copy here, and I can't very well let you have that.'

'Get somebody in the place to type them,' said Lowe, 'and have them sent to me at Portland Place by special messenger. I'll pay all expenses of course.'

'All right, sir, I'll do that,' agreed the local inspector.

Lowe thanked him and took his leave. Shadgold followed him out to the waiting car.

'Have you got any doubt about this fellow, Smedley, being the right man?' he asked.

'Candidly, no,' answered the dramatist, 'but you heard what I promised his brother?'

'You're only wasting your time, Mr. Lowe,' said the Scotland Yard man, shaking his head. 'We've got all the evidence we want for a conviction, and you won't find any of the other sort.'

'I quite agree with you,' said Lowe ruefully, 'but I've promised and there you are.'

They shook hands and the dramatist took his place behind the wheel.

'When are you coming back to London?' he asked as he slipped the gear lever out of neutral.

'Maybe to-night, anyway to-morrow morning,' replied Shadgold. 'I'll look you up when I do.'

He waved his hand as the big car glided away, watched it out of sight and went back to rejoin Lightfoot.

Trevor Lowe arrived in London shortly after eleven and found his secretary, Arnold White, engaged in sorting over the morning mail.

'Hullo, sir!' he greeted. 'I see by the paper that the villain of the piece has been rounded up. It doesn't mention you, by the way, but I conclude that you had something to do with it.'

Lowe helped himself to a cigarette.

'A little but not much,' he remarked. 'However, I haven't finished with the business yet.'

White looked round interestedly.

'What's in the wind?' he said. 'Isn't the guilty man guilty after all?'

'I don't think there's any question of that,' said the dramatist, blowing out a cloud of smoke. 'No, it isn't that.'

He proceeded to tell White what it was.

'I see,' remarked the secretary when he finished. 'What chance is there of finding a loophole in the evidence against this chap?'

'About one in three million, I should say,' retorted his employer. 'I'll tell you all about it.'

He pulled a chair up to the fire and sat down.

'Now listen,' he said, 'and if you can find any flaw in the evidence against Smedley, I should be glad if you'd point it out.'

Slowly and in detail he recounted everything that had been discovered while he was at Hill Green, and White listened attentively. At the conclusion he shrugged his shoulders.

'It seems a clear case to me,' he remarked.

'So it does to me,' agreed Lowe. 'There isn't one single point where it's possible to establish a case for the defence.'

'There's just one,' said Arnold White after a thoughtful pause. 'I don't suppose it would lead to anything but it's worth trying.'

'What's that?' inquired the dramatist.

'That broken nail,' answered White. 'You might see if it fits the broken nail on Smedley's finger.'

Trevor Lowe sat up suddenly.

'That's one up to you, White!' he exclaimed. 'I never thought of that.'

White looked rather pleased with himself.

'I expect you'll find it'll fit all right,' he said.

'I've no doubt of it,' said the dramatist. 'But it's a good suggestion and worth trying. Look up the number of Hill Green police station and get on to Shadgold.'

The secretary complied and a few seconds later turned from the desk with the receiver in his hand.

'Here you are, sir,' he called. 'Inspector Shadgold's on the phone now.'

Lowe went over and put the black cylinder to his ear.

'Hullo, Shadgold,' he said. 'I want you to do something for me and let me know the result.'

'What is it?' asked the Scotland Yard man over the wire.

'I want you to find out,' said the dramatist, 'if that piece of nail we found coincides with the missing piece on Smedley's finger. Will you do that, and phone me?'

'Yes, if you think it's going to be of any help,' was the reply.

'I don't,' said Lowe frankly. 'But White suggested the idea, and it would be interesting to see.'

'All right, I'll try it and let you know in a few minutes,' said Shadgold

Lowe hung up the receiver and turned to his secretary.

'Shadgold is going to test your idea and we shall have the result in a few minutes,' he said.

He lit another cigarette and they waited in silence. Neither expected anything from this test of the broken nail, and yet admitted to themselves that there was a possibility. The time went by, five minutes stretched into ten, ten into fifteen, and then the telephone bell rang persistently.

Lowe crossed to the instrument.

'Well, Shadgold?' he said, and there was another silence while the man at the other end of the wire spoke rapidly.

Watching, White saw Lowe's face change. An eager look replaced the almost expressionless one with which he had gone to the telephone. Presently he spoke.

'I'll be down in about an hour and a half,' he said. 'There may be nothing in it, but I'll come all the same. Don't trouble to send the copies of those reports, I can see them when I arrive.'

He hung up the receiver and walked over to the fire-place.

'Well?' asked Arnold White.

Lowe looked at him queerly.

'Pack your bag and get the car round,' he said. 'We're both going down to Hill Green at once. That shred of nail found in the fur collar of Miss Mortimer's coat does *not* fit the torn nail on Smedley's finger.'

20

The Compact

There is a small shop in Hill Green which in any other neighbourhood would have been referred to as a café or a restaurant, but which, since Hill Green had to be different at all costs, was called the Tea House.

It was quite a small establishment and run by two angular maiden ladies of uncertain age, who regarded the few customers they ever got with malignant expressions from behind a screened-off portion of the shop that served as an office. The Tea House was never very full, for the residents of Green Hill preferred taking that soothing and cheerful beverage in the privacy of their own houses, and the single waitress was never very busy.

This particular afternoon was no exception, for, apart from the table at which Mr. James Bryant sat frowning and glancing at the door, only one other was occupied. The two women who had been drinking tea when he had entered had continued to sit on smoking and gossiping, much to the young man's annoyance, for he had hoped to find the place empty, or at any rate that the two women would go as soon as they had finished their tea.

Joyce, too, was late — a good twenty minutes — and he was beginning to get impatient. He had already stalled the waitress by saying he was waiting for a lady, and he felt rather a fool that the expected lady had not materialized.

He crushed out the stub of his second cigarette and was feeling for a third when the door opened and Joyce Elliot came in.

She was smartly dressed as usual, but under the small hat her face looked pale, and the pallor was accentuated by the dark rings under her eyes.

Jim rose as she came towards him, and at the same time became conscious that the hissing flow of gossip from the table occupied by the two women from Hill Green had ceased. It had ceased suddenly, like the turning off of a tap, and from the corner of his eye he saw that they were surveying Joyce with open curiosity. The waitress too was gazing at the newcomer with open-mouthed interest.

Jim's colour was a little heightened as he greeted the girl. Of course, these people had heard that her uncle had been arrested that morning, and looked upon the girl as an interesting exhibit.

'I'm sorry I'm late, Jim,' she murmured as she sat down in the chair he pulled out for her and began to strip off her gloves. 'But Pops has been a little trying.'

'That's all right, dear,' said Jim quickly. 'You'd like some tea, wouldn't you?'

He beckoned the still staring waitress. Joyce nodded. 'Please,' she said.

The waitress came over to take the order with alacrity.

'Tea for two,' snapped Bryant, 'and — ' He looked across at the girl. 'Toast or something?' he asked.

She shook her head.

'Nothing for me, thank you,' she said.

'Just tea,' continued Jim; and when the waitress had drifted away to give the order: 'Now what's the idea of this conspiratorial meeting?'

Joyce smiled — not a very successful attempt, but still undoubtedly a smile.

'I wanted to talk to you,' she said, 'and I thought this place would be quiet.' She looked round. The two women with heads very close together were whispering excitedly. 'I wanted to talk to you about Uncle Harold, and what we ought to do,' the girl went on.

'What do you mean?' asked Jim.

'Well, we must do something,' said the girl quickly. 'We can't just sit down and do nothing.'

'I don't exactly see what else we can do,' he replied.

'What we can do is to prove that he's innocent,' said Joyce.

Jim looked at her in surprise.

'Oh!' he said. 'How can we do that?'

'By finding out who really did commit these murders,' she answered.

Jim's expression was a little dubious.

'I don't see how we're going to do that,' he remarked.

'Neither do I at the moment,' said

Joyce. 'That's what we've got to discuss.'

The waitress brought the tea, and they waited until she had gone.

'It seems to me,' said Jim as Joyce poured out the tea, 'that it's going to take a jolly lot of discussion.'

'It's not going to be easy,' admitted the girl. 'But somebody committed these crimes, and I'm going to find out who it was.'

She handed him his cup, and he took it with a little worried frown.

'I suppose,' he said hesitantly, 'I suppose you are quite — I don't like to say it, dear — '

'You mean, am I quite certain that Uncle Harold is not the murderer?' she broke in calmly. 'No, I'm not certain of that at all. I'm quite willing to admit that he may be, but I'm fair enough to give him the benefit of the doubt, which, under the circumstances, is more than the police and a jury will.'

'And you can scarcely blame them with the evidence against him,' said Jim.

'I'm not blaming them any more than I'm blaming you for believing him guilty,' said Joyce. She stopped him with a gesture as he opened his mouth to protest. 'You know you do think he's guilty so what's the good of denying it?'

'I'm afraid,' he confessed, 'that I do — much as I would like to think otherwise.'

'There you are, you see,' she said. 'So somebody has got to keep an open mind if they're to help him. That's just what I'm trying to do, and what I want you to do.'

'What exactly do you want me to do?' he asked.

'I'll tell you,' she said and pushing aside her cup, she leaned forward. 'I want you to try and believe that Uncle Harold is innocent. I want you to forget the evidence against him, and that experience in his past.'

'That's a little difficult,' he said.

'I know it is,' she went on quickly. 'But I'm trying to do it myself. I'm saying to myself Uncle Harold is innocent. He didn't kill Doctor Wallington; he didn't kill Miss Mortimer; he didn't kill that man Tidd. He's not 'The Hangman.' I've been saying it ever since this morning, and I'm beginning to believe it.'

'Supposing you are,' he said as she paused, 'what good is that going to do?'

'It's going to do this good,' she answered. 'If we start from the point that Uncle Harold, in spite of appearance, isn't the murderer, then the murderer is still at large, and to save Uncle Harold we've got to find him.'

'The police — ' he began.

'The police will do nothing more,' she said impatiently. 'They believe they have got the man, and they won't look further. And if Uncle Harold ever comes before a jury, he'll be convicted. The only hope is that somebody — outside the police — can find the real murderer, and that's you and I.'

'You suggest that we take up the rôle of amateur detectives?' said Jim.

'Yes,' she nodded. 'I suggest that we go on as if Uncle Harold didn't exist — as if the mystery was still unsolved — and see if we can find anything out. Must I do it by myself, or will you help me?'

He hesitated for a moment, and then

against his better judgment, he nodded.

'I'm with you,' he said. 'When — and how — do we start?'

She flashed him a grateful look, and he wished heartily that the Tea House had been completely deserted.

'We can start at once,' she said. 'How — I can't answer that quite so easily.'

She smiled ruefully.

'I've read quite a lot of detective stories,' said Jim, 'and the proper procedure in these cases is to look for the person who benefits by the death of the victims.'

'How are we going to do that?' asked the girl.

'I think you'd better leave that side of it to me,' said Jim. 'I've got a friend who's a reporter on the *Post-Courier* and has access to all sorts of information. I'll run up to town and look him up in the morning. He may be able to give me some information regarding the private lives of these people. That will help us.'

'I think that's a good idea,' said the girl approvingly. 'What can I do?'

Jim wrinkled his brows in thought.

'I think the best thing you can do,' he

replied, after a short pause, 'is to make a list of all the people who could have got hold of that key to the gardens. Try and find out when the three keys were last seen together, and then make a note of the people who called at the house after that, and were in a position to pinch one.'

'That's splendid!' she cried enthusiastically. 'We're getting on, aren't we?'

He nodded. He wasn't at all sure where they would get to, but he did not tell her that. And it was just as well he did not know, for their interference was destined almost to cost Joyce Elliot her life!

21

A New Angle

Lowe and Arnold White arrived at Hill Green well within the time the dramatist had stipulated, and having, to the open surprise of the staff, booked rooms at the 'Hillside Hotel,' went straight on to the police station. A rather perturbed Shadgold was waiting for them in the charge-room.

'You know, Mr. Lowe,' he said after they had shaken hands, 'you mustn't set too much store on this nail business. If you come to think of it, Smedley's nail would have had time to grow. So it isn't really extraordinary that the piece we found in Miss Mortimer's coat doesn't fit.'

'I've thought of that,' replied Lowe. 'That's why I've come down. So far as I can see, what we want to prove is whether that scrap of nail came from Smedley's finger or not.'

'Which,' grunted the stout inspector, 'is

not going to be so easy.'

'I don't think it's going to be difficult,' answered Lowe; 'in fact, I think we can test it at once. I've brought the necessary apparatus with me.'

Shadgold raised his eyebrows.

'What are you going to do?' he asked. 'You can't do anything that will damage that piece we've got. We shall want to put it forward as evidence.'

'I'm not going to injure it in any way,' replied the dramatist. 'I merely want to borrow it for a quarter of an hour, together with a paring of one of Smedley's other nails.'

He took an oblong mahogany case that White was carrying and stood it on the table.

'This is a microscope,' he said. 'I hired it from an optician's on my way down. It's a very powerful one and a glance at the two pieces of nail ought to tell us what we want to know.'

The Scotland Yard man looked a little anxious.

'Not a very convincing proof, is it?' he asked doubtfully.

'I think you'll find it most convincing,' said Lowe.

'Well, there's no harm in it so far as I can see,' said the inspector. 'What is it you want? Our bit of nail and a fresh bit of nail from one of Smedley's fingers?'

Lowe nodded, and Shadgold turned to Lightfoot.

'Will you see about that?' he asked.

The local inspector gave a grudging consent. Clearly he thought the whole proceeding a waste of time. While he was gone, Shadgold watched the dramatist unpack the mahogany box, assemble the microscope and set it up under the light.

'The result of this experiment should lead to rather interesting conjectures,' he said, 'that is, if the nails do not correspond.'

'I don't think there's much likelihood of that,' grunted the inspector. 'If you've got any idea in the back of your head that Smedley is the wrong man, you're making a big mistake.'

'I haven't any such idea,' replied Lowe. 'I've no ideas at all at present. I'm merely following up White's suggestion.'

Lightfoot came back, and approaching the dramatist, held out his hand.

'Is that what you want, sir?' he said.

In the palm was a small shred of nail.

'That's exactly what I want,' said Lowe, and picked it up between his finger and thumb. 'You are prepared definitely to identify this nail paring as having come from one of Smedley's fingers?'

Lightfoot smiled rather sourly.

'Certainly I am,' he answered, 'seeing as I cut it off myself.'

'Right,' murmured the dramatist, and put the scrap carefully between a cover glass.

This he placed on the stage of the microscope, and adjusted the mirror, so that the light was concentrated on the small object. Applying his eye to the eyepiece, he slowly twisted the milled wheel that controlled the focus until it was sharp and clear.

'Now take a look at that, Shadgold,' he said, straightening up.

The Scotland Yard man looked.

'Great Scott!' he ejaculated. 'Is that a piece of Smedley's nail? It looks like a bit of Mount Everest!'

'It's Smedley's nail all the same,' replied Lowe.

He invited Lightfoot and White to look through the eyepiece, which they did.

'Now,' he went on when they had finished, 'let us compare that with the piece that was found in Miss Mortimer's fur collar.'

Lightfoot went into his office and returned with the piece of nail in a small box. Lowe took it and put it under the cover glass beside the other piece. Once more he looked through the microscope, and they heard his breath hiss through his teeth as he drew it in sharply.

'Well?' asked Shadgold.

'Well?' said Lowe, and his face held a peculiar expression. 'I am willing to go before any jury and swear that these two pieces of nail do not belong to the same man.'

There was a silence.

'Nonsense!' exploded Shadgold. 'They must!'

The dramatist shrugged his shoulders.

'Look for yourself,' he said.

Shadgold bent down and peered through the microscope.

'They certainly don't look alike,' he admitted, 'but that's probably because they were taken from different fingers.'

'It's nothing of the sort,' said Lowe. 'It's because they did not come from the same man. Smedley's nail is a finer texture. The nail taken from Miss Mortimer's coat is very coarse. You can see that.'

Shadgold ran his hand through his close-cropped hair.

'But it's absurd,' he protested. 'Do you realize what you're inferring? That by a most extraordinary coincidence, both Smedley and the murderer have each lost a piece of finger-nail. It's too impossible to be taken seriously.'

'I agree with you,' nodded Lowe. 'It is.'

Shadgold stared at him irritably.

'I don't see any other explanation,' he grunted.

'There is another,' murmured the dramatist.

'I should like to hear it,' said the inspector.

'You shall,' said Lowe. 'As you say, it's

absurd to believe for one moment that this nail business is a coincidence. It's about a million chances to one that it should be. Particularly with all the other evidence against Smedley. The only other explanation, therefore, is that the whole thing is a 'frame-up.''

Shadgold's jaw dropped and his eyes almost started from their sockets.

'A frame — ' he began. 'What the dickens are you talking about?'

'A frame-up,' explained Lowe, 'is an American expression — '

'Damn it!' shouted Shadgold. 'I know what it means! What I want to know is how can it be a frame-up?'

'If it is,' said Lowe, and his face was very grave, 'it's one of the cleverest and most diabolical things that have ever been done. And it means that you have not yet caught the man who calls himself 'The Hangman.''

'It's impossible!' broke in Lightfoot. 'Do you mean that someone deliberately left that nail in Miss Mortimer's coat in order to throw suspicion on Smedley?'

Lowe nodded.

'Yes,' he answered, 'and more. Some-body knew Smedley's past history, and planned these crimes with that in his mind. Don't you see the cunning of it? This unknown person wanted to get rid of Doctor Wallington and Miss Mortimer. He knew that Smedley had come to live at Hill Green, and planned everything so that it should look like the work of a lunatic, knowing that sooner or later Smedley's identity would be discovered, and that he would be suspected of the crime. The clues left were not too blatant, just sufficient to serve their purpose with-out looking as if they'd been left intentionally.'

Lightfoot looked at Shadgold with a worried frown, and Shadgold rubbed ner-vously at his moustache.

'Aren't you taking a lot for granted, Mr. Lowe?' muttered the Scotland Yard man. 'After all, you're making a lot out of a very little — '

'Shadgold,' interrupted Lowe, 'yester-day I was as convinced as you were that Smedley was the guilty man. To-day I am almost equally as convinced that he is innocent. It's that' — he pointed to the microscope — 'that has changed my opinion.'

'There may be some mistake — ' began Lightfoot, but the dramatist shook his head.

'There is no mistake,' he said stubbornly, 'and anyway, you can take the opinion of experts on the matter. Both these pieces of nail can be sent up for examination, and I'm sure that the report you will receive will correspond with what I say.'

'Smedley said he'd torn his nail in putting on his overcoat,' grunted Shadgold, 'but of course, we didn't believe him.'

'And yet I'm almost sure he was speaking the truth,' said Lowe.

The inspector pinched his chin gloomily.

'If you're right,' he grumbled, 'it means we've got to start all over again.'

'Yes,' agreed the dramatist, 'but with the possibilities narrowed down. What you have to look for now is a man with the following qualifications.' He checked them off on the fingers of his left hand as he spoke. 'One, he must have known that

Harold Nethcott was Harold Smedley. Two, he must have had access to the Nethcotts' house, and known of the torn finger-nail. Three, he must be the possessor of a cool, clever and cunning brain; and four, he must have had some strong motive for wishing the deaths of Doctor Wallington and Miss Mortimer — '

'And 'Monkey' George,' put in Shadgold, 'don't forget him.'

'I think he was killed because he knew too much,' answered Lowe. 'He was a poacher, wasn't he, and rather a bad lot from all accounts? It seems to me more than likely that he stumbled in some way on the identity of this hanging man, and tried to turn his knowledge into money, instead of telling the police.'

'That's quite possible, sir,' agreed Lightfoot. 'It's just the sort of thing 'Monkey' George would have done.'

'This is a bit of a facer, Mr. Lowe,' said Shadgold, 'and I don't mind telling you that I'm a bit uncertain what to do. I can't let Smedley go, that's definite, and yet you've made me feel that the fellow may not be guilty after all.'

'Why not leave things as they are for the moment?' suggested Lowe. 'If 'The Hangman' thinks that his plan has succeeded it will give him a sense of confidence. In the meanwhile, you can go quietly to work, and try to find out the truth. It would be a good plan, I think, to discover who has access to Nethcott's house. If you can get a list of all these people you'll probably find the murderer among them.'

Later on that afternoon Jim Bryant made the same suggestion, unaware that the police were going to work along similar lines.

22

The Knife in the Dark

'Among your list of the murderer's qualifications, Mr. Lowe,' said Shadgold, 'you forgot to include the fact that he must also have a portion of nail missing from one of his fingers.'

'I didn't forget it,' replied the dramatist. 'I think it's very possible he has. I don't see where he could have got hold of the piece that was left in Miss Mortimer's collar in any other way.'

He had removed the two scraps from the cover glass and put them in the little box. This he handed to Shadgold.

'You'd better lock that up carefully,' he said. 'It would be a good idea if we drew up a short statement regarding the result of the experiment this morning, and all signed it — '

He broke off as the police surgeon came into the station.

'Hullo,' said Doctor Murford with raised eyebrows. 'I thought you'd gone back to town?'

'Not yet,' said the dramatist, and went on with his occupation of repacking the microscope.

The little doctor's sharp eyes saw it.

'Have I interrupted a scientific lecture?' he remarked with a sneer. 'Really, this is remarkably interesting. It's so like all the fiction I've read.'

'Most fiction,' said Lowe, 'has a basis of fact. Ask Inspector Shadgold and he will tell you that the laboratory at Scotland Yard is most amply equipped.'

'Is that so?' said Murford, and shrugged his shoulders. 'How's your prisoner this morning?' he asked, turning to Shadgold. 'That's what I really came in about.'

'He seems to be all right. Why?' grunted the stout inspector.

He did not like Doctor Murford and took very little pains to conceal the fact.

'Merely the natural anxiety of a doctor for his patient,' replied the other. 'I've been treating him for some weeks for general debility, and I don't suppose the

217

shock of his arrest has done his health any good.'

Trevor Lowe looked up quickly.

'Are you the Nethcotts' doctor?' he inquired.

'I am,' said the police surgeon shortly.

'You must have seen a good deal of Harold Smedley lately?' went on the dramatist.

Doctor Murford eyed him a trifle suspiciously.

'Certainly,' he replied. 'Why?'

'I was wondering,' said Lowe, 'whether you had formed any ideas as to his mental condition.'

'I'm not a brain specialist,' was the retort, 'so I'm afraid I must decline to answer that question. In any case, my opinion would not be worth anything. If you want a report of his mental state you must engage the services of an alienist.'

'I was only asking you for an opinion,' said the dramatist. 'By the way, how is your hand? Is it better?'

'My hand?' Murford stared at him.

'I was under the impression that you had injured your hand,' said Lowe smoothly. 'One of your fingers, wasn't it?'

The doctor took his left hand out of his pocket and looked at the neat finger-stall. 'It's practically healed,' he said. 'I nearly cut the top off with a bread knife.'

He turned his back deliberately on the dramatist and addressed himself to Shadgold.

'I should like to see Smedley,' he said. 'Have you any objection?'

Shadgold shook his head reluctantly.

'I've no objection,' he said. 'Have you?' He glanced at Lightfoot.

'No,' replied the local inspector. 'I'll take Doctor Murford down.'

'Thanks,' snapped the little doctor, and he and Lightfoot went out through the door that led to the cells.

'Unpleasant fellow, isn't he?' grunted Shadgold.

Lowe smiled.

'I'm afraid Doctor Murford is rather full of — Doctor Murford!' he said. 'I'd certainly like to have a look at that injured finger of his. The bread knife explanation is certainly a good one, but it may not be true all the same.'

'It looks a bit suspicious to me,' admitted the Scotland Yard man.

'I think it would be advisable,' said the dramatist, 'to keep an eye on Doctor Murford. He may be as innocent as a babe unborn; on the other hand he may not. He was friendly with the Nethcotts and therefore has one of the qualifications possessed by the murderer.'

'And he was a constant visitor to the house,' said the stout inspector musingly. 'But it's going a bit far to suspect the divisional-surgeon of being a murderer.'

'At the present state of the case,' said Lowe, 'I should suspect anybody and everybody, if I were you.'

He picked up the mahogany box containing the microscope and handed it to Arnold White.

'I'm going to get some lunch now,' he said, 'and I shall be at the 'Hillside Hotel' all the afternoon if you want me.'

'What about those reports?' asked Shadgold. 'Do you still want them?'

'Yes, have they been typed?' said the dramatist.

The inspector shook his head.

'No, but you can have the originals if you like.' He went into Lightfoot's office and came back with a sheaf of papers. 'Bolton was going to do these this afternoon,' he said, handing them to Lowe, 'but there's no need now if you can let us have them back by to-morrow morning.'

'You can have them back this evening, if you want them,' said Lowe, and a few seconds later he and White took their leave.

After lunch Lowe settled down before the fire in the hotel lounge to wade through the reports dealing with the private lives of Doctor Wallington and Miss Mortimer, but he found very little to repay him for his diligence. Doctor Wallington had had no money at all except what he made from his practice, and Irene Mortimer, though a little better off, had had an income that was so microscopic that it was hardly worth taking into consideration. Murder for gain, then, seemed to be improbable. Both of them had left wills. Miss Mortimer had left all her property to a

Mrs. Barlow, an old school friend. And Doctor Wallington had bequeathed his books and instruments, which were all he had to leave, to another doctor named Slack, who had a practice in Greater Linden, which adjoined Hill Green. They were both distant cousins of a Mrs. Conner, a woman apparently of wealth and position who lived in Knightsbridge, and that was all the reports had to offer. Not the slightest suggestion upon which even the hypothesis of a motive could be based.

Trevor Lowe smoked and worried over the matter throughout the entire afternoon, and he was still worrying when White, who had gone out to see the beauties of Hill Green, came back for tea.

After tea the dramatist read the reports again in the hope that there might be something he had overlooked, but without result. He spent the evening in verbally going over the entire affair with his secretary, but when he had finished he found it had not advanced him the fraction of an inch. At eleven o'clock he decided to go to bed, but although he felt tired, it was a long time before sleep came. Lying staring up at the dim white of the ceiling, he tried to work the thing out. It was the motive that was the stumbling block. Once he could get an inkling of that, he felt that the rest would be easy. It was after one before his eyes closed and consciousness left him . . .

In the dark and shadowy corridors of the hotel silence reigned. There was a glimmer of light from the lounge where the night porter nodded in his glass box, but apart from that there was no sign of life. The old-fashioned grandfather clock ticked monotonously, and somewhere in the region of the kitchens the intermittent nibbling of a rat at the wainscot broke the stillness of the sleeping house.

The clock ticked on, and presently, with a preliminary grunting, chimed two. The porter roused himself at the sound, looked sleepily about him, and relapsed once again into semi-consciousness. The noise of the nibbling rat seemed to grow louder, faded and abruptly stopped. There followed after an interval the faint creak of a floor board which mingled with the gentle snore of the now-sleeping porter. The door leading to the kitchens moved. Very slowly it began to open — widening inch by inch until there was room for a dark and stealthy form to slip through into the passage. It came cautiously and noiselessly, this thing born of the night, came forward until it reached the foot of the wide shadow-swathed staircase. It wore a long coat that reached nearly to its heels, and where normally there should have been a face, was nothing but a patch of blackness. Through the holes in the mask the man's eyes glittered as he watched the dimly seen figure of the sleeping porter. He began to ascend the stairs, testing each before trusting his full weight upon it. He reached the first landing, paused and listened, and then made his way softly down the righthand passage until he came to the door of Trevor Lowe's room. Here he stopped, peered at the number to make sure, and then stooping, tried the handle. It turned, and pressing against the door, he found to his satisfaction that it was unlocked. He opened it a few

224

inches, and looked in. The room was in pitch darkness but he could hear the regular breathing of its occupant. His gloved hand dipped beneath his coat, and came out holding a long, thin knife. He tested the razor-sharp edge, and a mirthless grin curled his lips beneath the mask. Cautiously he advanced towards the bed, guided by the deep breathing of the sleeper . . .

Lowe stirred uneasily, and opened his eyes. Darkness surrounded him on all sides, and he could hear no sound, but in that moment of waking he was conscious of danger. The purely animal instinct which during waking hours is so often swamped by reason, was alive and active in that transition state before the conscious mind had regained complete control. He turned his head, and at that moment something sharp and cold pricked his throat!

23

A Near Thing

It was sheer luck that saved his life. The point of the knife had actually pierced the skin of his throat, when there came a long and unmusical snore from the next room. The sound so startled the killer that his hand jerked the weapon aside, and in that second Lowe acted. Rolling sideways, he threw himself off the bed, clothes and all, and landed in a heap on the floor. He heard a muttered oath, and while he was trying to extricate himself from the enveloping folds of the sheet and blankets, the sound of scurrying footsteps and a banging door.

There was a considerable lapse of time before he was able to free himself, and scramble to his feet, and as he raced to the door a sudden shout came from below, followed by a scream of pain and the thud of another slamming door.

Racing along the corridor to the head of the stairs, he hurried down into the lounge, and the first thing he saw was the night porter, white-faced and clasping his wrist from which the blood was pouring.

'I tried to stop 'im!' gasped the man. 'But 'e 'ad a knife.'

He reeled and Lowe gripped him by the shoulder.

'Steady,' said the dramatist, 'let me look at that wrist of yours.'

The porter held out his arm. The wound was a nasty one, but not particularly dangerous, and with the man's handkerchief, Lowe improvised a rough bandage.

'You'd better get on the phone to the nearest doctor,' he advised, 'and also the police. Which way did he go?'

'Through the kitchens, sir,' answered the dazed porter.

Lowe went over to the communicating door and pulled it open. Beyond, the rooms lay in darkness, but he felt for the switch and found it. A blaze of light drove away the gloom, and looking quickly round, he saw that the place was empty. A closer inspection showed the way by which the night visitant had got in and made his escape. Opening off the big kitchen was a large scullery, and wash-house. The window which overlooked the garden at the back of the hotel had been forced and was now wide open. There were several traces on the sill where the man had scrambled over, and on the floor beneath was a cake of mud which had evidently dropped from his shoes. Lowe went back to the lounge and found an alarmed and sleepy-eyed manager, and White. They demanded to know what had happened.

'I've had a visitor,' said Lowe grimly. 'A most unpleasant gentleman who tried to cut my throat.' He fingered the scratch on his neck tenderly.

'Good God!' squeaked the manager. 'A burglar?'

'You can call him a burglar, if you like,' said the dramatist, 'but I've got a worse name for him.'

He turned to the porter as the man came dazedly out from his little glass box.

'Did you phone the police and the doctor?' he asked.

The man nodded.

'The police are coming along at once, sir,' he replied, 'but the doctor's out. 'E 'ad a night call. I've left word for him to come 'ere as soon as he gets back.'

'Which doctor was it?' snapped Lowe quickly.

'Doctor Murford, sir,' said the porter. ''E's the nearest.'

Lowe frowned.

So Murford was out, was he? It might only be a coincidence, of course. The manager, a little recovered from his first shock, was taking charge.

'You'd better wake up the servants,' he said to the porter. 'We must find out if anything's been stolen — '

'Nothing has been stolen,' interrupted the dramatist. 'The man who broke in did so with only one object, and that was to kill me.'

The horrified manager gaped at him.

'To kill you?' he repeated stupidly. 'Why should he want to kill you?'

'Because he thinks I'm going to be a nuisance,' said Lowe, 'and he's right! I'm going to be a damned nuisance!'

'Do you know who it was then, sir?'

asked the manager, and the dramatist nodded.

'I don't know what he calls himself in private life,' he retorted, 'but publicly he's known as 'The Hangman!''

The manager's fat face became the colour of lard, and he uttered a little squeal of terror.

''The — the Hangman?'' he gasped huskily. 'Good God — here!' And then as a sudden thought struck him: 'But they've got 'The Hangman' at the police station.'

'They've got Harold Smedley at the police station, which is not the same thing at all,' said Lowe. 'White, get my torch, there's a good fellow.'

The secretary hurried away, and Lowe, after a glance at the porter, turned to the shivering little manager.

'Is there any brandy you can get at quickly?' he asked. 'Because if there is, you'd better give your porter a good stiff glass. He's not only had a nasty shock, but he's wounded as well.'

'I've got some in my office,' said the manager, and fumbled in the pocket of his hastily-assumed trousers for his keys. 'I'll get it.'

He unlocked a door beside the reception desk, and entered the room beyond. Presently he came back with a bottle and glasses.

'Perhaps you'd like some too, Mr. Lowe,' he suggested as he poured out two stiff drinks.

The dramatist shook his head.

'No thanks,' he answered.

The manager gave a glass to the porter, who gulped it down eagerly, and swallowed the contents of the other himself. A little colour came back to his flabby cheeks.

'That's better,' he breathed, as he set down the empty glass, and looked round as Arnold White came hastily down the stairs.

'Here you are, sir,' he said, and Lowe took the torch he held out.

'I'm going out into the garden,' he said, crossing to the door that led to the kitchen. 'You may as well come with me.'

The secretary followed with alacrity.

'So that's how he got in,' he remarked as he saw the open window.

'And that's how he got out,' said Lowe,

unfastening the back door. 'Perhaps we can find some more traces of him in the garden.'

They searched the place thoroughly and by a low brick wall that divided the garden from a narrow lane they found in the soft mould of a wide flower-bed several deeply printed footmarks.

'That's where he got over,' muttered the dramatist.

He looked over the wall, paused for a moment and then hoisted himself up. The lane on the other side was very narrow, and ended in a door in the wall. Lowe dropped to the ground and flashing his light before him, walked towards the point where the lane joined the road. He found nothing in the lane itself, but out on the road near the entrance was a little pool of black oil. The man had evidently come in a car and left it standing there. He found nothing else, and coming back, once more climbed the low wall, and rejoined White in the hotel garden.

'Found anything?' asked his secretary, and Lowe shook his head.

'Nothing of any importance,' he replied.

'He came by car.'

'This pretty definitely clears Smedley, doesn't it?'

'So far as I'm concerned, it does,' said the dramatist, 'but it wouldn't convince a jury, I'm afraid. They'd argue that there was no proof that the man who attempted to kill me was 'The Hangman.''

'And there isn't, either,' remarked Arnold White.

'That's true,' agreed his employer. 'But it couldn't have been anyone else.'

'I suppose you wouldn't be able to recognize him again?' asked the secretary.

'No, I scarcely saw him at all,' answered Lowe. 'The room was dark.'

'Perhaps the porter can help,' suggested White. 'The lounge was lighted and he must have been pretty close to have got wounded.

The porter, however, could offer no assistance.

'I never saw his face, sir,' he declared. ''E 'ad it covered with some black thing, an 'andkerchief it looked like.'

'What build was he?' persisted the dramatist.

The porter scratched his chin, and shook his head.

'I couldn't tell you, and that's a fact, sir,' he said frankly. 'It all 'appened so quick like, that I was fair bowled over. I couldn't tell you what 'e was like.'

He stuck to this statement later when questioned by Shadgold and Lightfoot. The stout inspector, hastily dragged from his bed, and minus his collar and tie, arrived with Lightfoot ten minutes later. He listened with a wrinkled forehead to Lowe's brief account of the night's happenings.

'And the fellow got away?' he commented at the finish. 'Pity, that. I wish you'd caught him. If I'd been here — '

'If you'd been here he'd probably have stopped to breakfast,' snapped Lowe irritably. 'Realizing that he had nothing to fear.'

Shadgold reddened.

'There's no need to be rude, Mr. Lowe,' he remonstrated, and the dramatist's face cleared.

'I'm sorry, Shadgold,' he apologized, 'but this business is getting on my nerves.'

He saw the surprise in the Scotland Yard man's face and went on quickly:

'It's not this attempt on my life. It's the whole thing. Everything seemed plain sailing and easy at first, and it's turned out to be nothing of the sort. The murderer is still at large, and for all we know, waiting to pounce on a fresh victim. The horrible part of it is, that if he is we can't stop him. We haven't the faintest clue to his identity. All we're sure of, and we can be pretty sure of that, is that he isn't mad. But that's all, we don't know anything else.'

Shadgold scratched his chin with a stubby finger.

'I suppose there's no doubt that it was 'The Hangman' who came to-night?' he remarked.

'Not the slightest, so far as I'm concerned,' said Lowe. 'He's got to hear, in some way, that we've realized that the case against Smedley is a frame-up, and this was his effort to put me out of the running. If he'd succeeded he'd probably have had a go at you too.'

Shadgold frowned.

'How could he have heard?' he said. 'We haven't told anybody.'

The dramatist shrugged his shoulders.

'You can't keep things dark in a place like this,' he answered. 'All the local police have got wives, and they talk.'

He yawned.

'There's one thing, if our friend knows that his plans regarding Smedley have gone wrong, he's had a shock, and that may do some good. If he panics he may do something to give himself away.'

His words were truer than he knew. The man who called himself 'The Hangman' was in something very near a panic, for he had not only received one shock that day, but two.

24

Missing!

Jim kept his promise to Joyce on the following morning and he was in a frame of mind that was by no means free of pessimism. He travelled up to Town by car, and having left the vehicle in the care of a City garage went on foot to seek out his Fleet Street friend.

He found him doing nothing in particular, in the big newspaper building in which he worked, and he came to Jim in the waiting-room.

'No, I'm not busy at the moment,' he said after greetings had been exchanged. 'What's up?'

Jim persuaded him to come out to a nearby hostelry and drink beer, and over the beer he explained his errand.

Dick Warren whistled into his tankard.

'You've cut off a large slice of trouble for yourself, haven't you?' he grinned.

'I've read up all about the Hanging Murders, and I don't think there's much doubt of this fellow's guilt.'

'I don't think so either,' confessed Jim. 'But I'm in a rather difficult position. I can't very well refuse to help.'

The other nodded sympathetically.

'No, of course you can't, old chap,' he agreed. 'But I don't think you'll accomplish much. However, anything I can do I will, and what you want is pretty easy.'

He drained the tankard and ordered two more.

'I can probably get all the information you want from the office,' he added. 'If you come along back there with me I'll see.'

Jim thanked him, and after the beer had been gratefully consumed, walked back to the offices with his friend. An hour later he was in possession of as much information concerning the victims of the murderer as the police.

'Who's this woman, Conner?' he asked, as over lunch, which he had insisted on sharing with Dick, he read through the various items they had succeeded in collecting.

'Elderly, a widow, and very rich,' answered the reporter laconically. 'Lives in a big house in Knightsbridge, and seldom goes outside the door.'

'And she was related to these people?' said Jim, wrinkling his brows. 'I suppose there's no chance of getting a glimpse of the will?'

'Her lawyer might let you, but it's doubtful,' said the reporter shortly. 'Why?'

'I was just wondering' — Jim helped himself to some more cheese — 'to whom she's left her money.'

'Don't see how that's going to help you,' argued Dick. 'Supposing she'd left it to Wallington and Mortimer, they won't get it; and, anyway, she's still alive.'

'It's only an idea of mine,' explained Jim rather apologetically. 'I was wondering if there couldn't be something like this: Supposing this woman, Conner, has made a will leaving her money to Wallington and Mortimer, with a clause that if they should die before her the money goes to somebody else? Supposing this somebody else knows that and bumps off Wallington and Mortimer, with the intention of later on bumping off the lady with the money? That would supply a motive.'

Dick Warren sat up quickly.

'By Jove, young Bryant!' he exclaimed, 'that's darned smart!'

'I've dabbled a lot in law,' said Jim modestly. 'Was going to read for the Bar at one time.'

'Look here,' said Dick excitedly. 'Mrs. Conner's solicitors are Rushton & Small, of Lincoln's Inn. Let's go round there. I'll come with you and see if we can find anything out.'

Jim agreed, and finishing their coffee quickly he paid the bill, and they went out. A taxi deposited them at the door of Messrs. Rushton & Small, and a dried-up looking clerk took Dick's card into the august presence of Mr. Lester Rushton, the only surviving member of the firm.

After a short interval they were ushered into the private office of the solicitor. Mr. Lester Rushton frowned at them over his steel-rimmed glasses. He was an aged man, and seemed to have absorbed a great deal of the dust that surrounded him. His voice when he spoke crackled like ancient parchment, and his skin looked as though it would have been most useful to engross a lease on.

'Mr. — er — Warren,' he said, glancing at the card between his fingers.

'That's me,' broke in Dick. 'I'm afraid, Mr. Rushton, that we've come on a most unconventional errand, and you will when you hear it probably order us out of the office.'

The solicitor raised his thin eyebrows.

'That,' he said, 'is not a very propitious beginning. At the same time I can assure you that I have listened to a great many — um — unconventional stories in this office. Supposing you start by sitting down?'

They sat down, and Dick began at once.

'You have a client, I believe,' he said, 'who was distantly related to the people who were killed at Hill Green — '

Mr. Rushton made a gesture and checked him.

'You are referring to Mrs. Conner,' he said. 'The lady is a client of mine but if you are seeking any information regarding her I'm afraid I cannot help you. I have already supplied the police with all the information that lies in my power.'

'I don't want to use this for publication,' said Dick hastily. 'I have really called to see you on behalf of my friend here, Mr. Bryant, who is interested in the case.'

He proceeded to tell the solicitor just how interested Jim was, and their reason for coming to see him. Mr. Lester Rushton listened in silence, and when Dick had finished, frowned, removed his glasses and wiped them carefully. For a long time he remained silent, and then he leaned back in his chair and looked at Dick.

'I'm afraid,' he said, with a slight shake of his head, 'that I cannot show you my client's will without her express permission. You will understand that it would be most unprofessional. But I can assure you that your — um — friend's theory is not tenable. Mrs. Conner's property was willed to be equally divided between Doctor Wallington and Miss Mortimer, but in the event of their decease before her the entire property goes to the London and Suburban Hospital for Cancer Research.' Mr. Rushton's face broke into a cracked smile. 'I'm sure,' he added, 'that you can hardly suspect the hospital of being concerned in the deaths of these two unfortunate people.'

'And that's that,' said Dick, two minutes later, as they walked towards the Strand. 'It was a good idea, young Bryant, but there's nothing in it.'

Jim Bryant went back to Hill Green feeling rather dispirited. That flash of inspiration at lunch had raised his hopes, and he had seen himself going back to Joyce with the problem solved, or, if not exactly solved, at least with someone whom they could suspect. But now it appeared as if there was nothing else to do but accept the police theory that Harold Smedley was guilty after all. There was definitely no other motive except insanity.

Jim had no means of knowing that the police were even at that moment revising their original theory, and were by no means as convinced of Smedley's guilt as they had been. He had left too early in the morning to hear about the attempt on Trevor Lowe's life, and it was not until he called round to the Nethcotts' house that evening that he heard of it.

He found Francis Nethcott rather worried and perturbed.

'Hallo, Jim!' said the little man as he was shown into the drawing-room. 'Have you seen Joyce?'

'Seen Joyce?' echoed the young man. 'No, not since yesterday afternoon. Why?'

'She went out early this afternoon,' said Mr. Nethcott, shaking his head, 'and she hasn't been back since. I waited dinner for over half an hour for her.'

'Perhaps she is dining with some friends,' suggested Jim.

'She isn't,' declared the other. 'I thought that at first, and then I thought it funny she hadn't phoned — she always does — and I rang up the only people she would be likely to be with and none of them had seen her.'

Jim felt a little thrill of apprehension run through him.

'Did she say where she was going when

she went out?' he asked.

Mr. Nethcott nodded.

'She said she was going for a spin in the car,' he replied. 'Which undoubtedly she did, for I sent down to the garage and the car had gone.'

'Then she may have had a breakdown,' said Jim, and felt a tinge of relief. 'That's about what has happened.'

He helped himself to a cigarette with a hand that trembled slightly. For a moment he had imagined unnameable things.

'I hope you're right,' replied the little man gloomily. 'I can't help feeling worried all the same.'

It was then he told Jim about the attempt to kill Trevor Lowe.

'But this lets your brother out, surely,' exclaimed the young man. 'They can't hold him after that.'

'That's what I thought,' agreed Mr. Nethcott. 'But apparently there's no proof that this man who broke into the 'Hillside Hotel' was 'The Hangman.' I believe the police are beginning to have their doubts about Harold's guilt, but they're not going to release him.'

'Anyway, it looks better for him than it did,' said Jim.

He remained chatting until both men, realizing that the girl was still absent, and that it was getting late, fell into an uneasy silence. The clock pointed to eleven when Nethcott, who had been pacing restlessly up and down, suddenly stopped.

'Something's happened to her,' he said huskily. 'I'm sure of it. There's nowhere she could be all this time unless something had happened.'

Jim tried to reassure him, although he was feeling thoroughly alarmed now himself, but Nethcott would not listen.

'If she isn't here by half-past eleven, I'm going to inform the police,' he declared.

Half-past eleven came and went, but no Joyce came with it, and the little man, pale and frightened, went out into the hall and picked up the telephone receiver.

'Give me the police station,' he said in a voice that shook, and a few seconds later was speaking rapidly to Inspector Lightfoot. While he did so, Joyce was wondering, helplessly, how long she had got to live!

25

The Hangman!

When Joyce Elliot announced her intention of going for a drive in the car, that was exactly what she had intended doing. She had spent the morning thinking over her compact with Jim and wondering exactly how best she could start her campaign to prove her uncle's innocence. This had been more difficult than she had imagined, but she had started by making a list of all the people who had had access to the house during the past month — she thought that was taking it back far enough — and a formidable array of names it was.

She counted them and found they totalled twenty-six, including the servants. And not one of the twenty-six was, so far as she could tell, likely to be responsible, or have any reason, for killing Doctor Wallington, Miss Mortimer or

'Monkey' George.

She felt it was a very good beginning, and hoped that Jim would have better luck with his friend the reporter. If only they could light on some possible motive, seventy-five per cent of their task would be completed.

She studied the list again after lunch, and was possessed of a wild idea to close her eyes and stick a pin in it at random. She suppressed this desire, however, and, coming to the conclusion that a little fresh air would do her good, made up her mind to take the car out.

The garage — a somewhat glorified title for the shed which housed the car — was only a short distance from the house, and she soon had the machine out and was heading away from Hill Green towards the open country.

There was a spot almost twenty miles away that Joyce particularly loved. The road wound its way up a steep hillside between woods to an open space from which it was possible to see for miles round.

The view was really beautiful, and when she reached the top of the hill she pulled up, intending to pause and smoke a cigarette. She found her cigarettes all right, but no matches. There was usually a box kept in one of the pockets on the doors, but she searched in vain, and then she remembered that the police had overhauled the car, and guessed that they had taken the matches.

Her guess was quite unjustified really, but she grew unreasonably annoyed. There was just a possibility that there might be a box in the tool compartment under the seat, and, getting out, she pulled up the cushion of the driving-seat to open it.

Something dropped as she did so, and fell on the floorboard with a little tinkle.

Stooping she picked it up. It was the broken half of a cuff-link. For a moment she thought it was one of Pop's or her uncle's, and was slipping it into the pocket of her coat when she recognized it.

It belonged neither to Francis nor Harold Nethcott, and as she realized the significance of her discovery the blood receded from her face and left her dazed and pale.

There was no doubt that this car had been used by 'The Hangman' when he had killed George Tidd. The police had made certain of that by comparing the tyre-marks at the cross roads, and it was one of the pieces of evidence against her uncle. Then the owner of this broken piece of cuff-link was 'The Hangman,' and she knew him!

With shaking limbs she got back into the car and sat behind the wheel, staring with unseeing eyes at the view which was wont to give her so much pleasure.

She had accomplished her task. By a piece of inconceivable luck she had found the murderer. There was no mistaking that piece of cuff-link. It was distinctive, and the person who owned it had never openly been in the car.

Everything fitted. She could see with startling clearness one of the names on the list, the name of the man to whom that link belonged. The first shock of her appalling discovery began to wear off, and she found herself thinking rapidly and clearly.

Should she drive straight back, and

inform the police, or should she follow up this clue, that Fate had almost thrown in her lap, herself?

For a long time she sat motionless, trying to make up her mind, and eventually she decided.

She would not go to the police. Not yet, at any rate. If she did, her suspect might succeed in clearing himself. He was clever enough to find an explanation for that link being found in the car, and then he would not only be warned, but take precious good care that all other possible clues were destroyed.

No, she would follow this up herself, and at once. As she started the engine and slowly let in the clutch, she wished that Jim had been at home, so that she could consult him; but still, she would, at any rate, have something to tell him when he came back.

Swinging the car round, she drove back towards Hill Green and the house of the man whose broken link reposed in her pocket.

★   ★   ★

Joyce Elliot awoke from what seemed like an unpleasant dream. Her mouth and throat were dry and her head was aching terribly. She looked about her into utter darkness, and was for a minute or two puzzled to know what had happened to her, and then she remembered.

The finding of the broken cuff-link — her decision to follow up the clue herself — the growing suspicion of the man with whom she had had tea — the sudden dizziness after that last cup, and then oblivion.

She was lying on something soft, and when she tried to move she found that her wrists and ankles had been bound. The dryness of her mouth and throat was due, she discovered, to a gag that had been tied securely about her lips. She could see nothing, but she guessed where she was. In the house of the man she had been so foolish as to visit alone.

How he had become suspicious of her she could not tell, but concluded that her questions had not been as clever as she had believed. That cup of tea — her second — had without a doubt been drugged. She remembered that he had made an excuse to leave the room just before it was poured out. He had gone, of course, with the intention of getting the drug.

Curiously enough, she felt no fear, and wondered at herself. She put it down to the fact that her senses were still dazed by the drug she had swallowed, for there was certainly cause to fear. The man into whose clutches she had fallen would stop at nothing to ensure his safety, and she was, while she lived, a distinct menace to that safety. His action in treating her as he had was sufficient proof of his guilt, and for his own sake he dared not let her go back to the world and tell her story.

In a detached way, as though she were considering the case of somebody else, she speculated on the method he would use to kill her. Would he treat her as he had treated the others? She rather hoped he wouldn't. There was something dreadful at the thought of being hanged.

A twinge of pain in one of her legs made her wince, and she moved with difficulty to try and ease the cramp that was attacking her. She succeeded in turning over on her side, and found a modicum of relief.

Everything was very silent and still, and she wondered what the time was. She had no means of telling, for she couldn't say how long she had been unconscious. For a long time she lay staring into the darkness, and presently found that she was hungry. This material craving almost made her laugh. It was so stupid to think about food when at any moment she might meet her death. And yet hungry she was, and would have given a lot for a good meal and a cup of tea.

She was dozing when the sound of soft footsteps made her alert and wakeful. They stopped close at hand, and she heard the clink of metal against metal. A cold draught of air blew into her face. There was the soft thud of a closing door and the click of a switch.

The darkness was suddenly dispelled in the blinding light of an electric globe which blazed overhead. In front of her, standing by the door through which he had entered, was the man to whom she owed her present position.

He advanced a few steps farther into the room and looked down at her.

'So you have recovered, eh, Miss Elliot?' he said pleasantly. 'I hope that the drug I was compelled to use has left no very unpleasant after effects.'

The gag prevented her replying, and he evidently required no answer for he made no attempt to remove it.

'I'm terribly sorry that all this should have been necessary,' he went on, 'but it was entirely your own fault, and I'm sure you will realize that under the circumstances I could hardly have acted differently.'

He might have been addressing a board meeting, so carefully did he choose his words, and so completely without emotion was his voice.

'It is a great pity,' he said shaking his head, 'that you didn't leave well alone, and keep out of this business. It is a most unpleasant affair. Nobody I'm sure finds it more distasteful than I do. But three people had to die for reasons which I need not go into, and one cannot pick and choose when the devil drives. But I am being quite honest when I tell you that I thoroughly dislike murder in any shape or form.'

Joyce stared at him, her eyes wide. There was no doubting that he was in earnest. He was merely speaking the truth. He had killed because for some reason it was necessary for him to kill, but he had done it much as he would clear up a nasty mess. There was something cold and calculating about this way of looking at wilful murder that sent a shiver of horror down the girl's spine.

Something of this must have been visible in her eyes, for the man before her smiled.

'You can't understand that, can you?' he said. 'You're shocked. You can't understand that, hating murder, I should yet commit it? There is no reason on earth why I should attempt to explain or justify myself to you, but I'm going to for my own satisfaction.'

He paused, pulled a chair towards her, and sat down.

'My argument is based on the fact that

most of us have to do things that we dislike in order to live,' he went on conversationally, 'and murder is merely a degree. I disliked having to kill Wallington immensely. In fact, it was quite a long time before I made up my mind to do it. I looked at the matter from all sides, and when I had come to the conclusion that it was necessary for my — shall I say comfort? — that Wallington should die, I set about killing him in the same way as I should set about selling a house — purely as a matter of business. Irene Mortimer was even more unpleasant, but that had to be done, and I did it. I arranged to throw suspicion on your uncle in order that I might remain unsuspected — again purely a matter of business — and a particularly clever piece of business, too, I think. George Tidd I felt no compunction in killing at all. All blackmailers should be killed. It is one of the unforgivable crimes. I don't know why I am telling you all this, but it gives me a lot of satisfaction to speak about it to someone who cannot use it against me.'

He stopped, and Joyce wondered to

what all this was leading. There was now no longer any doubt in her mind that this man, seated solemnly in front of her, was not sane.

His views were abnormal, warped, the products of a brain that had slipped just a hair-line over the border. He was not mad in the accepted sense of the word, not mad in the same way that poor Harold Smedley had been mad, but the possessor of a kink.

He rose to his feet and pushed back the chair.

'And now I'm going to tell you what I came to tell you,' he said, and there was no trace of emotion in his voice. 'Of course, you realize that having found me out, I can't very well let you go and give me away to the police. Neither can I possibly keep you a prisoner for ever, so I have only one alternative. You must cease to live.'

The girl on the low couch shrank back, and from behind the gag came a strangled cry. She had expected nothing else, but the shock was still the same.

He surveyed her pityingly.

'I'm really very sorry,' he said, 'and when I say that I'm speaking the truth. But in the position I'm placed it's essential. However, I have no intention of serving you the same way as the others. It is no longer necessary, for one thing, and besides, I've no desire for your death to seem anything else but an accident. There is, beyond Linden, as you know, a stretch of road bordered on one side by a sheer drop into a hollow.'

He looked at his watch.

'It is now a little after ten-thirty,' he went on. 'At midnight I shall come back, carry you out to your car, and drive you to that stretch of road. Some time during to-morrow you and the car — or what's left of it — will be found at the bottom of the hollow. I think the verdict at the inquest will be 'Accidental death.''

Without another word he went to the door, switched out the light, and she heard the key turn in the lock and his footsteps die away.

26

Escape!

Trevor Lowe sat in the charge-room of the little police station while Jim Bryant paced up and down, and Francis Nethcott leaned up against the mantelpiece and stared into the empty grate. Presently Shadgold came out of Inspector Lightfoot's office.

'The call has gone out to all stations,' he announced, 'with the description of Miss Elliot and the car. We ought to have some sort of news before midnight.'

The young man stopped his ceaseless patrol of the bare room and swung round.

'Ought we?' he exclaimed huskily. 'And is that all you can do, any of you? Just wait here until somebody rings up?'

'Steady,' said Lowe. 'We're doing all we can.'

Jim reddened, and then went white.

'I'm sorry,' he muttered.

'It's no good letting your nerves go,'

said the dramatist in a more gentle voice. 'I know how you're feeling but there's quite a chance that you may be worrying without cause. Miss Elliot may only have had a breakdown.'

'She would have telephoned if she had,' said Francis Nethcott dully. 'It's something more serious than that.'

'Whatever it is, we can't do any more than we're doing,' grunted Shadgold. 'We've telephoned all the garages, and warned all stations to look out for the car. That will be passed on to the patrols and point-duty men. If there has been an accident we should have news of it soon.'

Jim opened his mouth to say something, thought better of it, and said nothing. A silence fell, broken by the monotonous tramp of the young man's feet as he recommenced his pacing, and the loud ticking of the wall clock. Lowe stared at the floor and wondered. He had heard of their compact from Jim Bryant and he wondered if this absence of Joyce Elliot was even more sinister than any of them realized. Had the girl by some strange chance come upon a clue which the police had missed, and by so doing fallen foul of the murderer? It seemed to be the only alternative to an accident, and as Francis Nethcott had said, unless she had been very seriously hurt, she would surely have telephoned her home before this. He kept the alternative to himself, however. It would do no good to add to their fears, and nothing more could be done than was being done.

The stolid desk-sergeant stopped writing in his ledger as the telephone bell rang, and stretched out a long arm for the instrument. Four pairs of eyes fixed themselves on him as he lifted the receiver.

'Hullo!' he called, and then in a changed voice: 'Yes, sir, he's here now. Hold the line, sir.' He looked across at Lowe. 'The chief constable would like to speak to you, sir,' he said.

The dramatist crossed over to the desk, took the receiver from the sergeant's hand, and put it to his ear.

'Is that Mr. Lowe?' came Payton's voice over the wire, and then when the dramatist replied in the affirmative: 'I tried to get you at your hotel, but your secretary said you'd gone to the police station. Anything fresh?'

'Nothing,' said Lowe laconically.

'I thought I'd ring up and see if you'd found out anything about the fellow who attacked you last night,' said the chief constable. 'It's just come to my knowledge that an encampment of gypsies have settled near Linden, and these fellows are pretty desperate. I suppose it couldn't have been one of them?'

'It could, but I'm sure it wasn't,' broke in Lowe. 'I haven't the least doubt that the man who tried to kill me was 'The Hangman.''

There was a moment's pause.

'Well, it was only a suggestion,' said Payton at length, 'and as soon as it struck me I thought I'd ring you up. I'm just going to bed and if you've nothing to tell me I'll ring off.'

'No, I'm afraid there's nothing,' said the dramatist. 'We're all rather worried here at the moment about Miss Elliot — '

'Miss Elliot?' interrupted the chief constable in surprise. 'What's the matter with Miss Elliot?'

'She's disappeared,' answered Lowe. 'She went out this afternoon in her car, and she hasn't come back.'

There was an exclamation at the other end of the wire.

'Hasn't come back?' repeated Payton and his voice was suddenly concerned. 'Why, she left me at a little after five — '

'Did she come to see you then?' broke in the dramatist quickly.

'Yes,' was the reply. 'She called in the car round about four. I was rather surprised to see her because, although I've often been to the Nethcotts', she's never called before.'

'What did she call about?' Again Lowe interrupted him.

'About her uncle — Smedley,' answered Payton. 'She was terribly upset. In fact I thought she was going to be ill, but she recovered.'

'And she left soon after five?' said Lowe. He waved away Jim Bryant who was hovering at his elbow. 'Did she say where she was going?'

'No,' replied Payton. 'I naturally concluded that she was going home. I say, I hope nothing's happened. She nearly fainted while she was talking to me, and if she — I mean, if she felt ill again while she was driving her car — ' He left the sentence unfinished.

'They've warned all stations, anyway,' said Lowe, 'and if anything like that has happened we should hear pretty soon.'

'Well, you'll let me know directly you do hear anything, won't you?' said Payton anxiously. 'I feel rather worried. I ought to have insisted on driving her home myself.'

'I'll let you know at once,' promised the dramatist, and the other wished him good night and rang off.

Lowe hung up the receiver and turned to the others. In a few words he related the conversation he had just had.

'Called at Payton's did she?' said Mr. Nethcott. 'Well, that's something, anyhow.'

'It's nothing!' cried Jim, his face white and drawn. 'It only makes it worse. She left him at a little after five and it's now' — he glanced at the clock — 'a quarter past twelve. Seven hours and not a sign of her.' He dropped into a chair and covered his face with his hands.

'It certainly looks as though there's been an accident of some sort,' muttered Shadgold.

'Then she couldn't have driven straight home,' declared Trevor Lowe, shaking his head. 'If there'd been an accident between Payton's house and the Square we should have heard of it almost at once.' He fingered his chin and frowned. 'Where the devil can she have gone to when she left Payton?'

They looked at each other in turn, but no one offered a suggestion.

'Damn it, she couldn't have disappeared more effectively if the ground had opened and swallowed her up!' growled the Scotland Yard man. 'It's — ' He broke off as there came the sound of a sudden commotion from the passage at the back of the police station. 'What the hell?' he cried, but his words were drowned as the door was flung back with a crash and a man darted across the charge-room.

'Good God!' shouted Lowe. 'It's Smedley! Stop him!'

He flung himself in the way of the

racing man, received a violent blow on the chin, and staggered back. His foot collided with the base of the desk and he fell heavily to the floor. Before he could recover himself, or Shadgold could make a move, Harold Smedley had disappeared through the entrance to the police station into the night. The whole thing had happened so quickly that the stout inspector and the desk sergeant were taken completely by surprise. They recovered themselves however, and as Lowe scrambled to his feet they darted out of the door in pursuit. But the escaping man was already at the wheel of the dramatist's car which had been left by the kerb, and was frantically kicking at the self-starter. As Shadgold and the panting sergeant leaped down the steps the car began to move. Exerting all his energy, Shadgold ran forward and sprang on to the running board. His hands clutched at the side of the body, and then he received a heavy blow in the chest that sent him sprawling into the roadway. The sergeant helped him to his feet as the others came running out.

'He's got away!' panted Shadgold breathlessly, rubbing his right knee. 'Tell Lightfoot to phone for a car, we'll have to go after him.'

'How on earth did he manage to get out of his cell?' asked Lowe, and the stout inspector shrugged his shoulders.

'Heaven knows!' he grunted. 'Somebody's carelessness. We'd better go back and see.'

The car with Harold Smedley had disappeared into the blackness of the night as they turned and re-entered the police station. Inspector Lightfoot met them on the step looking worried and anxious.

'I want a car at once,' snapped Shadgold, and Lightfoot barked an order to the flustered sergeant.

A dishevelled constable was leaning against the desk, mopping at his nose with a large and none too clean handkerchief.

' 'E took me by surprise,' he said. 'Asked for a glass of water. An' when I brought it, 'it me on the nose, an' was out of the cell before I knew what 'ad 'appened.'

'Well, what we've got to do is to get him back again as quickly as possible,' growled the Scotland Yard man. 'Tell them to hurry up with that car, will you?'

It was fifteen minutes before the car could be obtained, but within four seconds of its arrival it was racing along the road in the direction taken by Harold Smedley.

And neither Shadgold, Lightfoot nor Lowe, who were in it, even so much as guessed what the night held in store.

27

Peril!

Lying in the darkness, with strained ears and thumping heart, Joyce heard those slow, measured footsteps fade to silence — a silence so great that the pounding of the blood which her wild heart was pumping through her veins sounded like a steam-hammer.

While the stranger had been speaking, she had scarcely realized the portent of his words. He had been so quiet and matter-of-fact that what he had said had been robbed of half its meaning. Now, however, that she was alone, full realization broke upon her like the suddenly released waters of a dam. If the threat that had been uttered was carried out, she had only a few hours to live! And she had no doubt that it would be carried out — to the letter. There had been something convincing in the very softness of his voice.

She frowned. Surely there was some way out! Over and over again she had read of the same kind of situation in books. She racked her brains to try and remember how, but she could think of nothing feasible. In the stories the hero had turned up at the psychological moment, but so far as she was concerned there was no hero to turn up either at the psychological moment or any other moment. Unless, of course, one could call Jim a hero. She smiled at the thought. Anyway, he did not know where she was, and was certainly not likely to guess.

Over and over again she wished that she had not been so foolish as to beard the lion in his den — or, at any rate, been less open regarding her suspicions.

If only she had gone to the police when she had found that cuff-link. Well, it was too late now — would, unless a miracle happened, be too late for ever.

She pulled herself up sharply, and found herself murmuring that well-worn cliche, 'while there's life there's hope.' Was there any hope? Was there any possible chance of getting out of this terrible position? She thought hard, staring into the darkness. Perhaps, if she could free herself from the cords that bound her, she would be able to find some way out of the room!

She set to work to try, twisting her wrists this way and that in the hope that the cords would loosen. But the man who had bound her had been careful over his job, and after ten minutes all she had succeeded in doing was to make her wrists sore. She lay still, feeling a little exhausted. A clammy perspiration had broken out on her forehead, and the atmosphere of the room seemed to have become unbearably hot. She knew that this was purely imagination, the result of overstrained nerves and panic.

Rigidly she schooled herself to control emotions. Panic would get her nowhere. After a little while she felt better, and set to work again to try and free her wrists. Clenching her teeth against the pain it caused, she strained her hands apart. The thin cords burnt into the flesh, but she thought that she felt them give slightly. If only they would stretch sufficiently to enable her to slip one hand free!

She redoubled her efforts, but her heart sank, and the momentary hope suffered eclipse. The cords may have given a little, or more probably she had imagined that they had, but they remained obstinately tight.

Panting and breathless, she was forced at last to rest. Once more in the silence of that oppressive room she almost gave way to panic.

The prospect was hopeless. There was really nothing that could save her from the fate her captor had planned. She tried to look at things logically and from a detached view-point. In a short space of time she, as Joyce Elliot, would cease to exist. She wondered if she would *know* when she ceased to exist. Would she be conscious of anything after death, or would she just go out — like a candle in the wind? She had heard many views expressed, but now, when the time was drawing so quickly near to actual knowledge, she found that none of them seemed feasible.

The muffled chime of a clock broke in

on her thoughts, and she began to count the strokes, but became uncertain half way through, and gave it up. She found herself wishing that the time would go quickly. If this was to be the end, she would rather get it over. This waiting was a dreadful ordeal — far worse, she was sure, than ever the reality could be. She was afraid that her nerves would give under the strain.

Obstinately and determinedly she tried to think of something else. Her school-days; little half-forgotten episodes and incidents that had occurred in her short life. Curiously enough, she found herself becoming absorbed in this retrospection, to the exclusion of the doom that menaced her.

And then she was brought back from the past to the present suddenly, roughly. It was the sound of the key turning in the lock that jerked her back and sent the blood pounding madly through her veins. She turned her head towards the door, and saw a dim light filter into the darkness as it opened. There was a click, and the room was ablaze with light

— light that threw up vividly the figure of the man she feared.

He advanced quickly and silently towards her, and, stooping, picked her up in his arms. She almost fainted with fright in spite of her determination to be brave, for she knew that the time had come.

28

Nothing to Chance

Major Wilfred Payton replaced the telephone receiver on its hook and smiled. The smile showed his even white teeth, of which he was inordinately proud, and also reflected his inward satisfaction. Major Payton was feeling extremely pleased with himself. That telephone message had been a touch of genius. It was a most natural thing for him, under the circumstances to have rung up Lowe and inquire if there was anything fresh, and the dramatist, as he had hoped, had introduced the subject of Joyce Elliot and so given him the opportunity of informing him that the girl had called at his house that afternoon — and left.

It was impossible to conceal the fact that the girl had been. His servant knew that because the man had admitted her. Payton had racked his brains for a long time over that problem and he had found a solution and such a simple one.

When he had discovered that Joyce knew a great deal more than she ought to know — and this had been absurdly easy, for the girl's questions had admitted of no mistake on that point — he had realized that some very drastic action must be taken if his own safety was to be assured. The drug he had administered was a harmless one, for then he had not decided what he was going to do with the girl — that had come after. But he realized that he had to act quickly, and he had done so.

As soon as she lost consciousness he had called Franklin, the man who attended to his wants, and sent off to the town for a restorative, and before the man had got back he had taken Joyce, bound and gagged her, and locked her in the small smoking-room adjoining his study. The car he had managed to squeeze into the garage beside his own — there was just room — and when Franklin had returned he had calmly informed the man that Miss Elliot had recovered and gone.

His telephone message to Lowe would bear out this story, and when the wrecked car was found no suspicion whatever would attach to him.

He glanced at his watch and lighted a cigarette. There was time yet, nearly an hour before he need start for the final scene of the drama — or rather the penultimate scene — for there would be one more, perhaps a week or a month later.

He poured himself out a drink, and carrying it over to a big easy chair, sat himself down at ease.

His schemes had been a long time maturing. Almost unconsciously his thoughts travelled back over the past months. It was difficult to say with exactitude when the first idea of murder had entered his brain. It had been such a gradual transition from the wish to the plan, and then the deed. At first it had been merely an idea over which he had pondered more to amuse himself than with any thought of actually putting it into practice, although the necessity was urgent and pressing enough, heaven knew. For Major Wilfred Payton,

D.S.O., Chief Constable for the county of Blankshire, had for the past year been face to face with ruin.

He was willing to admit, and did admit, for in that respect he was an honest man, that it was entirely his own fault. His love of gambling had brought him to the verge of bankruptcy, and eventually to the terrible crime of triple murder. There was a house near Park Lane which had seen him three nights out of the seven — a house innocent enough in its exterior, but within whose large and brightly-lighted rooms huge fortunes were nightly lost and won — won for the most part by the people who ran the place.

The ample fortune that he had inherited from his father had gone this way, and had been quickly followed by the large sums he had been able to raise from moneylenders.

Six months ago he had seen ruin and disgrace overwhelming him and had contemplated suicide. An appeal to his cousin, Mrs. Conner, had met with a blank refusal from that elderly lady and everything had looked hopeless. The three firms of moneylenders who held his promissory notes had threatened proceedings, and if that happened he knew it would mean his having to resign his position of chief constable. And then gradually had come the idea that had offered a way out.

It owed its inception to a remark made by Mrs. Conner at his second interview with her. He had made a last appeal, but the old lady had proved obstinate.

'No, Wilfred,' she had said, with a shake of her grey head, 'it's against my principles to lend anybody money. If you live long enough there's a very slender chance you may come into my property, but you won't touch any of it before.'

He had asked her what she meant, and she had replied:

'If anything happens to me my money will go to Alec Wallington and Irene Mortimer — equally distributed between the pair of them, but in the unlikely event of them dying before I do the whole of it will go to you. That's how I've made my will.'

Payton had left with blank despair in

his heart, and the letters he had found waiting for him when he got home had done nothing to raise his spirits.

They were peremptory, and not very civilly-worded epistles from the money-lending firms, giving him three months to redeem his promissory notes with a penalty of bankruptcy proceedings if he failed.

The total sum involved was in the region of 30,000 pounds, and Payton, if his life had depended on it, could not have laid his hands on 30,000 pence. And this to him was more than his life. It was disgrace and ostracism by the people of the county with whom he did, and wished still, to stand well.

As he undressed that night and sought his disturbed rest, he remembered he had wished fervently that some form of disaster would overtake his cousins and Mrs. Conner, and place within his reach the means of getting free of his troubles. But even then the idea of murder had not occurred to him. That was to come later, and it was to be inspired by an innocent inspector at Scotland Yard.

In the course of his duties as chief constable, Payton had visited the big building on the Thames Embankment, and after his business was completed he had been shown over the place. In the Record Office among many other photographs he had been shown one as a special curiosity.

'That's Smedley, the Hereford murderer,' said his guide, 'killed his wife and child by hanging them. The jury found him insane, and until recently he was shut up in Widemoore. You wouldn't think he'd kill anything to look at him, would you?'

Payton, his heart thumping wildly, made some conventional reply, for he had recognized the photograph as the brother of Francis Nethcott who had just come to stay with his brother at Hill Green. There was no mistake. He had been to the Nethcotts' to dine on the previous night.

'You say he was at Widemoore until recently?' he asked.

The inspector who was showing him round nodded.

'Yes, he's been let out now,' he answered. 'Supposed to be cured. His brother took him away.'

They passed on to other exhibits, but the information he had so accidentally learned kept flashing through Payton's brain. That night in the silence and darkness of his bedroom, the beginnings of the plan that was to develop into 'The Hangman' were born.

At first it was merely a wild idea that might be practical. Supposing Alec Wallington and Irene Mortimer were found hanged and supposing sufficient evidence was left that pointed to Harold Nethcott as the guilty man? With his record there wasn't a jury in existence who wouldn't bring in a verdict against him without leaving the box. He wouldn't suffer the extreme penalty of the law. They would be sure to say that he had never really recovered — that he was still insane and had broken out again. He would, at the worst, only be sent back to Widemoore.

The idea grew and became an obsession. With Wallington and Irene Mortimer removed only one other life — an old

283

woman — stood between him and fortune and relief from the worries that were tormenting him. If the first two could be removed without any suspicion attaching to himself the third stumbling block would surely be easy. A dose of poison administered after a lapse of time would settle Mrs. Conner.

He began to work the whole thing out in detail. By degrees it took shape as he added pieces until it was a concrete edifice without a flaw. The accidental sight of Harold Nethcott's torn nail gave him the idea of leaving a piece of nail behind as a clue. It was some time before he could make up his mind where he was going to obtain this necessary piece of nail. He could not take it from his own hand. That would be too dangerous because it would show. And then the solution had flashed on him. Of course! There was very little difference between a finger-nail and a toe-nail. A little special manicure and trimming was all that was necessary.

He had succeeded in obtaining an extension from the moneylenders, for now he had decided to put what had only been an idea into a practical fact, and having made all his plans, even to securing a duplicate key to the shed, where the Nethcotts' kept their car, he had killed Doctor Wallington.

It had been easier than he expected. He had made arrangements on the previous day for Wallington to meet him at seven-fifteen at the junction of Rose Lane and Meadow Road — a lonely spot at that hour. He asked him not to mention the appointment to anyone as it was connected with police business.

Wallington kept the appointment, and Payton met him in the Nethcotts' car, which he had surreptitiously borrowed for the purpose, using his duplicate key. If anybody had seen the car waiting and witnessed Wallington get into it, it would only have been another nail in the coffin of suspicion against Nethcott.

Payton had killed Wallington in the car, strangling him with the rope which he used after to hang him.

It had not been part of his plan to use the lamp-post on Milton's Rise, but the road had been deserted, and the idea had suddenly occurred to him. He had already provided himself with the card, and it had been easy to lift the body of his victim up until the loop of the rope had slipped over the bar on the lamp-post. It had only taken a few seconds all told, and then he had returned the car to the shed and gone home.

Irene Mortimer had been even more simple. He had known she was going to visit friends at Mrs. Topliss' and had waited near her home again in the Nethcotts' car. She had been surprised, when he called her to see him at that hour, but unsuspecting naturally had come near enough for him to seize her and pull her into the car. After that the rest was easy.

After the murder he had left the nail carefully concealed in her fur collar — he had originally intended leaving this clue on the body of Wallington, but had changed his mind.

Unfortunately for him 'Monkey' George had seen him enter and leave the barn, and demanded blackmail. Payton had dealt with him without a qualm, and — he smiled as he remembered this — it was the only one of his three crimes for which he had felt no compunction. He had hated killing poor Wallington and Irene Mortimer.

The putting of 'Monkey' George's body in the gardens in the centre of the Square had been the outcome of a piece of luck. Without any clear idea of how he was going to use it he had, on one of his visits to the Nethcotts' house, seen the keys hanging up in the hall, and taken one. After killing George Tidd he blessed his foresight, and used the key, throwing it away afterwards, so that it was sure to be found.

He had taken every precaution and left nothing to chance. In one respect fate had played into his hands. In the formulating of his plans it had struck him that when Mrs. Conner heard about the deaths of her cousins she might — remembering his financial state, and what she had told him — suspect something. It had been his intention to guard against this by seeing that she was too ill to take any interest in the happenings of the outside world.

There was a drug untraceable by the medical profession unless they were specially looking for it by which this could have been achieved, but nature had stepped in and saved him the trouble.

Mrs. Conner had caught a chill, and this had developed into acute influenza. She had been so ill, as a matter of fact, that Payton had been alarmed that she might die, and so effectually prevent his carrying out his scheme, for if she had done that it would have been too dangerous, even with the precautions he had taken for throwing suspicion on to Nethcott. Doctor Wallington and Irene Mortimer would have inherited the money, and the motive would have been too plain.

But she remained too ill to see anyone but the nurse and her doctor — who absolutely forbade the news of her cousins' deaths being told her — keeping just outside the danger list. By the time she was well enough to hear about the murders Payton had made up his mind to put the final part of his scheme into execution.

He finished his drink, and helped himself to another. Beyond a slight acceleration of his pulses, he was feeling perfectly cool. In fact, he prided himself that only once during the whole business had he felt anything else.

That was when he had learned of Lowe's experiment with the nail. He had almost given way to panic then. It had been panic that had sent him to the 'Hillside Hotel' in a futile attempt to put the dramatist where he could do no harm. It had been a mistake, and he realized it, for it had definitely proved that Harold Nethcott was not guilty, since he was locked up in the police station at the time.

Well, the unpleasant business was nearly over. He drank his second drink with a sigh of relief. He wished with all his heart that Joyce Elliot had kept out of it. He was not looking forward to what he had to do. But it had to be done, and there it was.

It was time now. He crossed to the door, opened it, and listened. The whole house was still and quiet. Franklin, his man, had been in bed for at least two hours, and the woman who came morning and evening to do the cooking had long since gone. Leaving the door open, he went into the hall and slipped into a coat, pulling a cap down low over his eyes.

Going back to his study, he went over to the door of the little smoking-room that adjoined it, and unlocked it. Switching on the light, he crossed over to the low couch on which Joyce was lying. This time he spoke no word, but, picking up the terrified girl in his arms, he carried her out into the hall. Laying her softly down, he listened again, and then began cautiously to undo the front door. The most risky part of his task was now to come. He picked the girl up again and carried her out into the cool darkness of the night, turned, and with difficulty because of his burden, gently closed the door.

The garage was round at the side of the house, and he took the precaution to walk on the strip of grass at the side of the path, so that his footsteps would make no sound.

With infinite care he opened the big door, and going inside, put the girl in the car. It was a peculiar characteristic of this man that he avoided looking at her, and the terror-laden eyes that followed his every action never once met his.

It was impossible to start the engine. He had to wheel the car out, and round to the drive. Fortunately for him, the drive ran down a slight slope to the road, and the car almost ran of its own accord. He got it into the road, and took his place behind the wheel. His heart was in his mouth as he started the engine, but his house stood by itself, and there was nobody to hear.

Slowly he let in the clutch, and the car began to move. As it glided along the dark thoroughfare a load lifted from his mind. So far so good. Another two hours at the most and he would be back, his task accomplished, and not a single breath of suspicion against him.

It was only a matter of a few days now before the reward for which he had risked so much would be his. He didn't know it, but he had taken all his risk for nothing, and steeped his hands in blood for a shadow!

A woman's prerogative of altering her mind had definitely put his reward out of his reach a fortnight after she had dangled the possibility before his eyes!

29

Through the Night

Payton drove with care. This was the one risky part of his whole plan. A description of the car had been broadcast, and if, by any unlucky chance he should be seen by a patrolling constable and stopped, it would be the end of everything — or the end of the constable. In the pocket of his coat he carried a fully-loaded automatic as a precaution against just this possibility. He hoped that it would not be necessary to use, for, strange as it may seem, Major Payton really had a distinct dislike of taking human life. What he had done — the crimes he had committed had been forced upon him. He was a proud man and the possibility of losing the prestige which he had laboriously acquired in the district around Hill Green, of being pointed out and whispered about by his friends and neighbours as a bankrupt, had been sufficient to break down this distaste for violence. But it was there. Even in the Army during the war he had hated the sight of death, and had never succeeded in becoming inured to it as had so many of his brother officers.

Psychologically, Major Wilfred Payton was a very curious mixture of contradictory characteristics.

He took a circuitous route in order to reach the road that would take him to his objective in order that he should not have to pass through the village, and the little car bumped and lurched over the rutted surfaces of the narrow lanes that he traversed.

How glad he would be when this night's business was over! He hated the whole thing! Why in the world had Joyce Elliot wanted to interfere? Why couldn't she have kept out of it and left him in peace, without inflicting this unpleasant and distasteful business on him? He felt a wave of annoyance pass over him. Everything had been planned so well and had gone so smoothly, and now, at the very last moment, this infernal girl had to butt in and almost spoil everything.

Well, it was a good job she had come to him instead of going to the police — or Lowe.

He swung the car round a sharp bend, and, crossing a secondary road, turned into what was little more than a cart track. He was driving here without lights, and twice he almost fouled the banks at the side. He would have to be more careful. An accident now would be an appalling disaster, and absolutely ruin all his carefully conceived plans. To his surprise, he found that the perspiration was running in streams down his face. He took out his handkerchief and wiped it away. This would never do. It was nerves, of course, but he mustn't give way to his nerves.

He had not done so far; it was silly on this, the last lap. This dark and twisting lane seemed endless, particularly at the slow speed he was forced to travel at, and yet he felt that he had chosen his route well. Except for the moment when he had crossed the secondary road, and at the very beginning when he had left his house, he had not gone near anywhere where he was likely to be seen.

Nobody would ever dream of looking for a car the way he had come. This was probably the first car that had passed that way in years. The surface was too bad and the way too narrow. The hedges on either side brushed against the car as he forced it through. He wondered if the branches would leave scratches on the paint and whether when the car was found at the bottom of the hollow these scratches would puzzle the police, and concluded that there would not be enough of the machine left to worry over that.

The narrow road began to widen and presently he came out on to a broad, macadamed highway. This was his real risky part of the journey. He dropped his right hand from the wheel, and feeling in his pocket, drew out the automatic, and laid it in his lap. He wasn't taking any chances. If anyone tried to stop him — well, so much the worse for them!

He swung round into the highway and pressed his foot on the accelerator. The car gathered speed, and, leaning forward, he switched on the lights. It would be better and safer to travel here with lights in case he met or overtook any other traffic. A lightless car would tend to rouse suspicion.

The engine purred rhythmically, and, responding to the pressure of his foot on the pedal, the car gathered speed. The headlights danced and quivered on the road ahead, and sprayed on to the hedges at the side, picking out the leaves in a bright emerald green. Payton's heart began to grow lighter as he decreased the distance to his destination. Another quarter of an hour — twenty minutes at the most — would see the end. Another hour and a half at the outside, and he would be back home and snuggling between the sheets, his task accomplished.

Suddenly he frowned and listened. Away behind him he heard above the gentle hum of his own engine the sound of another car. Slowing slightly, he glanced in the mirror attached to the windscreen. Behind him blazed two great white discs of light. Blindingly they blazed along the road, and even as he looked they drew nearer.

He increased his speed, but those circles of molten fire showed no sign of dropping behind. Payton muttered a curse. This was a nuisance. Whoever it was, they had a more powerful car than he, and it would be just as well to let them pass.

He was at the foot of the hill which led to the place he was making for, and it was essential that the other car should go by and get well away before he put his plan into execution. It would never do for anyone to see the car stop. When later they heard of the accident they might come forward and make a lot of trouble.

He decided on his course of action, and swerving to the side of the road slowed down. The great blinding lights swept nearer, and then the car was level with him. He expected it to roar past, and his heart jumped and he suddenly felt physically sick as it, too, slowed down and ran level.

And then he recognized it. It was Trevor Lowe's Rolls!

His teeth met in his lower lip until blood streamed down his chin. Had the dramatist found him out, after all? Was Lowe aware who 'The Hangman' was? Had he known all the time, and been playing with him like a cat with a mouse?

No, of course not. This was pure accident, but fatal for all that. Lowe must have been out for some reason and recognized the car. That was it. If he could get away, there was still a chance that everything would be all right.

He heard a shout from the big car, and took a quick glance at it as he increased his speed. The dashboard light was on, and in its rays he saw the face of the driver. Harold Smedley! Good God! But Smedley was in prison locked in a cell. Was he going mad? The wild face of the man in the other car couldn't belong to Harold Smedley. He opened the throttle to its fullest extent, and shot ahead, but only for a moment. The big, powerful machine that was chasing him drew level again. They were racing up the hill now, and at one side of the road was, as Payton knew very well — nothing!

And towards this side — the right hand side — the big car was slowly and relentlessly forcing the smaller one!

The sweat was running down Payton's face in streams and mingling with the blood from his bitten lips. His brain was working busily to try and hit on some plan to circumvent the other man, who was driving him to death. And then suddenly the car level with him shot ahead. Like a greyhound it bounded forward and silhouetted in the reflected glare of its powerful lamps, he saw it speeding away in front of him.

This new move puzzled him! What was Smedley up to? Had he given up and gone on? And then the meaning of the manœuvre flashed on him. Smedley was going to block the road!

Payton considered the possibility of turning and going back the way he had come, but discarded it almost as soon as he thought of it. The other car would overtake him easily — could overtake him even given a start. No — his hand touched the cold steel of the pistol on his lap — he would fight for it. It was very doubtful if Smedley was armed, and he would have the advantage.

A scheme came to him — a scheme that was simple and perfect in its completeness if he could carry it out. He would overcome Smedley and then send him and Lowe's car over into the void, together with the car containing Joyce Elliot. The whole thing would look natural. The two cars meeting on the narrow road, the collision, and both plunging over the precipice! So vivid was the picture in his mind that he could almost see it happening, and it would be better than his original idea — infinitely better. The pistol must only be used to scare Smedley. He mustn't shoot the man. That would spoil the whole plan.

The car in front, slowed, turned, and ran into the left-hand bank, forming an impassable barricade.

Payton set his teeth, gripped the butt of his automatic, and, bringing his own car to a halt, got out. As he did so, he saw Smedley advancing towards him.

30

Tragedy!

Harold Smedley sat exultantly at the wheel of Lowe's car. The cool wind blew against his heated face as he urged the machine forward and he could have shouted aloud at the sheer joy of it. He was free, free as the air that ruffled his hair and whistled past his ears.

Seated dejectedly in the little cell at the police station, his mind a chaotic whirl of doubt and fear, something had suddenly clicked in his head. An intense and savage desire to get away from the confining walls that hemmed him in took possession of him. He felt that unless he could get out he would have to beat his head against those stone walls.

He had experienced the same sensation once as a child when he had been shut up for some slight misdemeanour — the same craving for freedom. After that peculiar snapping in his brain his mental alertness seemed to have increased. It was as though a fog had rolled away and the plan by which he could escape had come to him like a flash. And he had done it!

His spirit sang as the car throbbed its way along the dark road. He had no idea where he was going and cared less. He only had a fierce desire to go on and on and on.

His foot pressed hard on the accelerator, and the car leaped and quivered like a living thing. The rhythmic purr of the engine was like music in his ears. His pale face was flushed, and his eyes, staring ahead at the road, revealed in the dancing splash of the headlights, were unnaturally bright.

He came to a turning and swung round almost on two wheels. He was in the main road now, a long stretch of smooth macadam with open fields on either side.

Staring at the black surface shining in his lights, all kinds of fragmentary scenes flashed and jostled each other through his brain. They had neither beginning nor ending, but unrolled before him like a crazy film. He was driving mechanically, without consciously knowing what he was doing, soothed by the hiss of the tyres and the steady purring of the engine.

And then suddenly in the glare of his lights he saw a car ahead. It was travelling at a good speed, and as he drew nearer he saw its number-plate, the white figures standing out sharp and clear-cut: XZ0360.

As he watched them they began to run through his head to a sort of tune: 'XZ0360 . . . XZ0360 . . . XZ0360 . . . ' It was peculiar. Why was it peculiar? XZ0360 . . . XZ0360 . . . XZ0360 . . . XZ03 . . . Of course! It was the number of his own car!

His own car? His brows drew together in a frown. Who could be using the car at this hour of the night? Not his brother. Through his crazed brain came a vague vision of Francis Nethcott. It must be Joyce, but why should Joyce be out so late? He was puzzled and being puzzled began to feel curious.

The car had increased its speed as though anxious to get away from him. He moved his foot, and brought it down harder on the accelerator. The great car bounded and quivered under him as he increased the speed. The receding number-plate of the car in front came closer. Above the roar of his own engine he could faintly hear the sound of the other. Steadily inch by inch he crept nearer, nearer yet —

Suddenly the car in front swerved and drew in to the side of the road. The move had been unexpected and Smedley shot by before he could apply his brakes. He came to a stop with a shriek from the protesting drums, and looked back. The other car was moving forward again, gathering speed. A moment or so and it would pass him. Whoever was driving it was apparently anxious to give him the slip. A wave of unreasoning anger took possession of him. He was going to see who was in that car. If it was Joyce, he would have something to say.

He released the brakes, and as the other machine drew level he shot forward and kept beside it. Behind the driving-wheel he caught sight of a white face glaring at him. A man's face that he seemed to know, but that had no right in that car.

He shouted, but the owner of the face took no notice, and Smedley felt his temper rise, and the blood began to hammer in his head. How dare the driver of his own car treat him like that. He swung in nearer, forcing the other car towards the side of the road.

They were running up a steep incline now, through wild and wooded country. At least it was wooded on one side; on the other there seemed to be nothing but blackness. Slowly towards this void he forced the smaller machine, and then he saw for the first time, pressed against the back window, another face — the face of a girl with wide, terror-filled eyes and something about her mouth that hid lips and chin.

Joyce!

What was she doing — like that? What was that thing bound round her mouth, and why did she look so terrified? The answer sprang to his mind, clear and illuminating. She wasn't in the car because she wanted to be. She was there because she couldn't help it. The thing about her mouth was to prevent her screaming.

He laughed, a harsh, mirthless sound that was blown back behind him and carried away on the wind. He knew now who the man was who was behind the wheel. Payton, the chief constable. He had got Joyce, and was taking her away — taking her away to that big house where they had shut him up for so many years — where they would have shut him up again if he had given them the chance.

'All right, my dear!' he screamed. 'Don't be frightened! I'll stop them! You shan't go!'

The rush of air drowned his words and scattered them to the darkness of the night. He would have to be careful now. He mustn't do anything to injure Joyce.

Dear little Joyce.

He frowned, forcing his aching head to think. He must stop the other car — that was what had to be done. Stop the other car . . . stop the other car. The spinning wheels made a rhythmic song of the words, and hammered them over and over again through his brain. Stop the other car . . .

And then he saw a way of doing it. The

road was narrow. He would get ahead and turn his own car until it acted as a barricade.

He gave a shout of triumph. That would do the trick. He let the car go all out, and it shot ahead. With a twist of the wheel he sent it rushing towards that well of blackness that bordered the road on the right, and then slowing he pulled the wheel hard round, and brought the car to a shuddering halt. With it's radiator touching the opposite bank, broadside on, it almost filled the roadway. Certainly there was no room for the other car to pass.

The driver evidently realized this, for he heard the squeal of his brakes as they were jammed suddenly on. He swung open the door and leapt out and as he advanced to the now stationary car Payton got out. Harold Smedley saw that his face in the reflected light from the headlamps was paper-white and twisted in a snarl.

'Move that car!' he rasped, and no one would have recognized his voice. 'Move it! Do you hear, or I swear I'll put a bullet through you!'

Smedley's eyes narrowed. He saw that

the other was holding a snub-nosed automatic.

'What are you doing with Joyce?' he said huskily. 'Where are you taking her — ?'

'Never mind what I'm doing with her?' snapped Payton. 'Move that car, as I tell you!'

With all the cunning of his crazy brain, Smedley pretended to hesitate.

'I don't think I can,' he said. 'The front wheels are jammed, and — ' He broke off, and his jaw dropped as he stared behind Payton. 'Look out!' he shouted suddenly. 'They're here!'

An old trick, as old as time, but Payton, his nerves on edge, fell for it. He swung round, and for the fraction of a second he was off his guard, and in that moment of time Smedley sprang.

With one hand he gripped Payton's pistol wrist and flung his other arm round his neck, jerking him backwards. The chief constable struggled hard, but Smedley seemed possessed of abnormal strength. Relentlessly he forced the muzzle of the pistol towards the roadway, and pressed hard on

Payton's trigger finger. With a staccato crackle, the magazine emptied itself harmlessly, the bullets pocking the surface of the road.

With a snarl of rage, Payton realized that the weapon was useless, and gave up his attempt to turn it against his opponent. Instead he flung his arms round Smedley and tried to trip him by lashing at the back of his heels with his foot. Smedley, his lips drawn back in a grin of rage and pain, counteracted this movement by wrenching one hand free and gripping Payton's throat. He got the man's windpipe under his thumb and pressed. Payton jerked his hand back, and tried vainly to get free, but Smedley followed up his advantage by bringing up his other hand.

He had his man by the throat now, and Payton, with the blood surging through his head and bursting lungs, tried in vain to loosen that deadly grip. He clawed at the other's wrists and battered at his white face, but all to no avail.

Backwards they staggered into the glare of the headlights. Their shadows, elongated and distorted, spilled over the road. A red mist was flooding before Payton's eyes. The noise in his head was like the thunderings of a thousand weirs. His swollen tongue protruded from between his parted lips. His attempts to struggle free were getting less and less — his thrashing arms more feeble . . .

Harold Smedley's breath was whistling from between his clenched teeth, but he made no other sound. Payton with a last supreme effort to break that stranglehold, twisted his legs round his assailant and flung himself backwards. The two men crashed heavily to the ground towards that black void on the right of the road. Almost to the brink they went, and — stopped.

The fall had loosened Smedley's grip, and Payton, drawing in great panting breaths to his tortured lungs, succeeded in tearing the other's hands from his throat. But his advantage was short-lived. Before he could scramble to his feet, Smedley had thrown himself upon him. The movement carried them both to the edge beyond which there was nothing.

A hoarse, inhuman cry broke from Payton's lips as he felt the solid ground drop away. A faint echo of that cry came up from the darkness of the void a moment later, and then — silence!

31

Dawn!

The police car raced on through the night. It was a good car, but not nearly so powerful as Lowe's own, and the dramatist was a little dubious of the chance of their overtaking Smedley, even if they ever caught sight of him. He had had a good start, and although at the moment could have gone by no other road than the one they were following, there was a mile ahead, according to Lightfoot, a junction of three roads, any one of which he might have chosen. When they reached this point Shadgold stopped the car and got out. In the light of a powerful electric torch the inspector examined the road surface for any marks of Smedley's tyres, but the ground was dry and hard, and he soon gave it up as useless.

'We shall have to choose one of these roads and risk it,' he grunted. 'There's no means of telling which one he took.'

'I'm afraid you're right,' agreed Lowe. 'But I suggest that you try the middle one. It's more probable that he would have gone straight on instead of veering either to the right or to the left.'

'The middle one leads through to Hinton,' said Lightfoot, 'the village is about five miles away and there's an A.A. box just beyond. The man in charge will be able to tell us if the car went by.'

Shadgold got back into the car and once more it went speeding forward into the darkness. Hinton was scarcely even a village. Its one street sloped sharply to the brow of a hill and down the other side, ending in a hairpin corner. At this point stood the A.A. box. The driver brought the police car to a halt, and the man in the box came out to them. The dramatist described his own car but the A.A. scout shook his head.

'There hasn't been a car of any description past here since ten o'clock,' he said.

Lowe thanked him and turned to Shadgold.

'We've struck the wrong road,' he said.

The Scotland Yard man nodded.

'The only thing to do is to go back and try one of the others,' he growled.

He gave the order to the driver and he backed the car and turned it. They roared back through the sleeping village and along the road to the junction.

'Which shall it be, sir?' asked the driver as they reached the point from where they had started. 'Right-hand road or the left?'

'Let's try the left,' said Shadgold.

The car swung into the left-hand road, and the driver put his foot down hard on the accelerator. The high hedges and the sentinel trees flew by, as with its white sword-like headlamps cutting a luminous path the car tore forward. This road seemed to be interminable: a long straight strip that unrolled over hill and dale. Suddenly the driver jammed on the brakes.

'What the deuce — ' grunted Shadgold, thrown forward in his seat, and then he saw why the man had made such a sudden stop.

A cyclist patrol was pedalling slowly towards them. The inspector signalled the man, and the policeman stopped, got off his bike and came over to the side of the car. Shadgold put the same questions to him as had been put to the A.A. scout. To his delight the policeman nodded a large and perspiring head. 'Yes, sir,' he said, 'a car like what you said passed me an hour or so ago up the road, goin' at a good pace it were, too.'

'That's Smedley,' said Lowe, and with a hurried word to the constable they started off again.

But luck was against them that night. They had not gone more than half a mile before with a loud explosion the right-hand back tyre burst. They carried a spare but it took them nearly fifteen minutes to fit it.

'I suppose we may as well go on,' grumbled Shadgold, as they climbed back again into the car. 'God knows where Smedley is by now, though.'

They went on, rushing through the silent night like a meteor. The country grew more wild and desolate, and presently the road narrowed as they reached the foot of a steep hill.

'Got to go carefully here, sir,' warned the driver, 'there's a sheer drop at the right-hand side of this road.'

He decreased his speed slightly, and then suddenly he gave a little grunt.

'What is it?' asked Shadgold.

'There's something ahead, sir,' muttered the man, and peering forward Lowe saw in the glare of the dancing headlights the bulky shapes of two cars.

'Must be an accident,' growled the inspector excitedly. 'Do you think Smedley has run into something?'

The dramatist made no reply, and the driver of the car increased his speed. Presently he brought it to a halt, with its radiator almost touching the number plate of the first car.

'Good God!' cried Inspector Lightfoot as he saw the white numbers on the plate. 'It's Mr. Nethcott's car!'

'That's the car that Miss Elliot went away in this afternoon,' said Lowe. 'There's something queer here. That's my car,' he pointed to the second machine drawn broadside across the road.

He got down, and followed by Shadgold and Lightfoot advanced towards the stationary cars.

They saw him pause by the first car, peer in through the side window and then pull open the door. His head and shoulders disappeared into the interior, then he straightened up and looked around.

'We've found Miss Elliot, anyway,' he said. 'Help me lift her out.'

Shadgold, at his elbow, gave him a quick look.

'She's not — ' he began, and the dramatist shook his head.

'No, no,' he answered quickly, 'but she's bound and gagged and I think unconscious.'

He glanced over his shoulder at Lightfoot.

'Will you get a cushion from the police car, Inspector?' he asked.

Lightfoot hurried away, and Shadgold and Lowe lifted the limp body of Joyce Elliot out of the car that had so nearly proved to be her coffin.

'She's fainted,' said Lowe, as they held her between them. 'I should think she's had a shock.'

'H'm,' grunted the stout inspector. 'I wonder who tied her up like this.'

Lowe made no reply, but signed for him to lay the girl down on the cushion which Lightfoot had brought. Bending over her, they removed the gag, and with Lowe's penknife cut the cords at her wrists and ankles. Her teeth were clenched and her eyes were closed, and she was breathing heavily, but was apparently unharmed.

'If we leave her in the air she'll recover,' said Lowe, and went over to his own car.

The front wheels were jammed into the bank at the left of the road, and the bumpers twisted out of shape, but otherwise the car was undamaged. There had obviously been no collision. The position the car occupied had been deliberately brought about. But what had happened to Smedley? Where was he, and the occupant of the other car? Obviously there had been an occupant, since the car was not capable of driving itself.

The darkness of the night was beginning to fade in the east. A greenish blue glow was spreading across the sky, a herald of the coming dawn, and the air was chill and sharp, laden with that peculiar sweetness which comes with the birth of a new day. It blew softly over the face of the unconscious girl and caused her to stir uneasily. Shadgold noticed the movement and called to Lowe.

'She's coming round,' he said.

The dramatist came over to the improvised couch.

'Now, perhaps,' he muttered, 'we shall learn what really happened here to-night.'

With a little sigh Joyce opened her eyes. For a moment she lay still, staring up at the velvety vault of the sky, and then as full consciousness flooded her brain an expression of terror crossed her face and she looked wildly about her.

'Oh!' The little cry, half choked and full of fear, burst from her lips and she struggled up on to one elbow.

Lowe dropped on one knee beside her and slipped his arm round her shoulders.

'It's all right, Miss Elliot,' he said soothingly. 'There's nothing to fear. You're quite safe.'

'Who?' she muttered hoarsely. 'Where is he?'

'Where is whom?' asked the dramatist gently.

'Major Payton,' whispered the girl. 'Don't let him come! Don't let him do it!'

'Payton!' The incredulous exclamation burst from Shadgold. 'What's she talking about, Mr. Lowe? What — '

The dramatist silenced him with a gesture.

'Why are you afraid of Major Payton?' he said.

'Don't you know?' she answered huskily. 'Don't you know that he's the man who's been killing all these people?'

'She's mad!' exclaimed Shadgold. 'Payton! Nonsense!'

'I'm not mad!' Joyce's voice was gaining strength. 'It's the truth I'm telling you. I found him out and went to see him . . . He drugged me and — and — ' She shivered. 'He was going to kill me, make it look like an accident, only Uncle Harold . . .'

Gradually they heard the story of the night, and listened with wondering faces. Payton! Payton 'The Hangman'! Even Shadgold was forced to admit at the end of the story that he doubted no longer.

'And they both went over together?' Lowe looked at the black void at the side of the road, now not so black in the grey light that was rapidly spreading over hill and valley.

Joyce nodded.

'Yes, I saw them,' she answered, 'and I heard them scream, and then I fainted. It was horrible . . . Horrible!'

Lowe rose to his feet, and with Shadgold by his side went over to the edge and looked down. It fell sheerly into blackness.

'We shall have to wait until it's quite light before we can do anything,' said Shadgold. 'I'll get Lightfoot to go back for help. Good God! Payton! It's — it's incredible!'

'Nothing in the world is incredible,' said Lowe, 'except the fact that people should any longer be capable of surprise.'

32

Odds and Ends

Inspector Lightfoot took Joyce with him to the police station at Hill Green, and having handed her over to the care of the delighted Jim and the equally delighted Francis Nethcott, came back again bringing with him two constables, men of brawn and muscle. The first cold yellow rays of the sun were sending slanting shadows across the scene of the final tragedy when they arrived. They had brought a rope and pulley tackle, and by the aid of these they were able to descend into the valley which formed the last resting place of Wilfred Payton and Harold Smedley. They lay, as they had fallen, locked in each other's arms, and both men were dead.

They were driven back to the mortuary in the police car, and by the time this had been done, and arrangements for the inquest settled, the morning was well advanced. It was lunch time before Shadgold and Lowe found time to sit down and take a breather.

'Well, that's the end of the business,' grunted the stout inspector as he swallowed half the contents of a tankard of beer in the lounge of the 'Hillside Hotel,' 'and I for one am jolly glad to see the last of it.'

'It wasn't a very savoury affair,' admitted Lowe, 'and there'll be the devil of a scandal. But it ended, I think, in the best way it could have ended. Smedley's brain was always unbalanced, and it's pretty evident, in spite of what the doctor's said, that he was never really cured.'

'I wonder if we shall ever discover what Payton's motive was,' remarked Arnold White.

'That's what puzzles me,' declared Shadgold, running his stubby fingers through his bristling hair.

'Unless it comes out in something you find among his papers,' said Lowe, 'I doubt if you'll ever know.'

In this he was wrong, for during the night Mrs. Conner had a serious relapse, and in the early hours of the morning, she died. The police, who knew of her connection with Payton, got in touch with Mr. Rushton, the solicitor, and from him learned as much of the truth as they were ever likely to learn.

'She apparently made a will,' said the solicitor, 'which I knew nothing about, leaving her property to Doctor Wallington and Miss Mortimer, and in the event of their deaths before hers, Major Payton. Apparently she changed her mind, for three months ago I drew up a will for her which followed the terms of the first as we know them now, but with this alteration: In the event of Doctor Wallington and Miss Mortimer predeceasing her, the property was to go to the London and Suburban Hospital instead of, as in the previous will, to Major Payton. The only explanation I can give for her changing her mind with regard to Payton is that she once remarked to me that she didn't feel certain he was a fit person to handle a large sum of money. She was rather an eccentric old lady, you know.'

It was Shadgold who brought the news to Trevor Lowe, and the dramatist listened gravely.

'Payton, of course, never knew that the second will existed,' he commented, and his mouth twisted into a smile. 'It's rather ironical when you come to think of it,' he went on. 'He took the greatest trouble, committed the dreadful crime of triple murder, all for the sake of enriching the funds of the London and Suburban Hospital to the extent of nearly a hundred thousand pounds!'

THE END

THE FACELESS ONES
GRIM DEATH
MURDER IN MANUSCRIPT
THE GLASS ARROW
THE THIRD KEY
THE ROYAL FLUSH MURDERS
THE SQUEALER
MR. WHIPPLE EXPLAINS
THE SEVEN CLUES
THE CHAINED MAN
THE HOUSE OF THE GOAT
THE FOOTBALL POOL MURDERS
THE HAND OF FEAR
SORCERER'S HOUSE

ROSE POINT

V. J. Banis

Karen marries Alan Denver and returns with him to the cliff-side house next to the lighthouse he tends. However, she knows nothing of the death — or even the existence — of his first wife. Then she begins to sense strange ghostly presences about the house, and her husband starts behaving oddly. She senses, too, that Alan's mother, who lives nearby, is trying to break up her marriage — but why? The truth lies hidden behind a locked door, and in a scrap of rose point lace . . .

THE CORPSE IN CACTUS

Lonni Lees

The murder that Detective Maggie Reardon has solved at a local Tucson art gallery creates unforeseen difficulties in her personal life. Then, to complicate matters, a corpse is discovered at a museum lying under a bed of cactus. What at first appears to be a tragic accident quickly starts to smell like murder. Maggie's been dealt a nameless victim with no witnesses, no suspect, and no apparent cause of death. And as the evidence unfolds, she must also battle a hostile fellow cop, determined to see her lose her badge . . .

MISSION OF MERCY

John Robb

A revolution breaks out in the independent Arab republic of Hanah. The French legation is in danger. A tiny Foreign Legion detachment is sent into the country, ordered to protect European lives and property. But that detachment is in no condition to undertake a task that calls for restraint as well as courage. It is under the command of Captain Laubert, a cunning but demented officer . . . a man who has been threatened with arrest by his junior officer.

THE ENVIED

John Burke

A dead scientist's undamaged brain is transplanted into a robot body and kept alive. Soon, other people who die in their turn come to inhabit the continually improving grey cases. But why do they sever all contact with their former friends and family members? Warren and his girlfriend Judith are both envious and suspicious of the way in which the Greys are taking control of society, and determined to discover their secrets. Then Judith dies and becomes a Grey . . . Five stories of the fantastic and the supernatural by John Burke.

SORCERER'S HOUSE

Gerald Verner

Sinister events in the village of Ferncross have given the inhabitants good reason to respect the legend surrounding derelict Threshold House: whenever a light appears in the window of the Long Room, they know from experience that a corpse will be found the next day. For two years the mystery has remained unsolved — until there comes a time when the killer strikes once too often. Because helping the police in their investigation of the latest murder is the unorthodox but astute Simon Gale . . .